DAN *and the*
SHARD *of* ICE

First published 2015 by A & C Black,
an imprint of Bloomsbury Publishing Plc
50 Bedford Square, London, WC1B 3DP

www.bloomsbury.com

Bloomsbury is a registered trademark of Bloomsbury Publishing Plc

A CIP catalogue for this book is available from the British Library

ISBN 978-1-4729-1245-9

Printed and bound by CPI Group (UK), Croydon, CR0 4YY

1 3 5 7 9 10 8 6 4 2

MIX
Paper from
responsible sources
FSC® C020471

DAN *and the* SHARD *of* ICE

THOMAS TAYLOR

A & C BLACK
AN IMPRINT OF BLOOMSBURY
LONDON   NEW DELHI   NEW YORK   SYDNEY

CONTENTS

For Kate Paice and Claire Jones,
with thanks from me and the ghosts.

I

THE GURU OF THE GUTTER

'But why must we see her, Daniel?' Simon waves his arm, sending clouds of ectoplasm scudding about his head. 'She is untrustworthy. The woman knows too much.'

'Yeah, well, that's precisely why we're seeing her,' I say, as we head further down the back alley. Wheelie bins and night shadows loom around us, and the lively sounds of the street fall behind. 'If anyone knows about poltergeists, it's Mrs Binns.'

'So you would rather take the word of a simple vagrant over mine?' Si looks appalled. 'I, who am your guide in this world and the next, and your best friend?'

I look at Si and take in his ragged eighteenth-century elegance, scraggy wig and skeletal features. Having a ghostly sidekick that only I can see is bad enough, but is he really the best friend I've got? Unfortunately, I've got a horrible feeling he might be.

'So what if she's a vagrant?' I say, steering the conversation back towards Mrs Binns. 'It's not like you to be so sniffy about someone down on their luck, Si.'

Si scowls at me, and puffs angry little clouds of ectoplasm out through the bullet hole in his head. I wonder, yet again, why he's so reluctant to see the old lady. She's helped us out before.

'Just be wary of her, Daniel,' he says eventually. 'She has a way of looking into your very soul and spying all your secrets there.'

'Secrets?' I say. 'What secrets do you have, Si?'

Si looks away and folds his ghostly arms.

'Let us just find the wretched woman and be gone from here,' he snaps. 'This place chills me to the core.'

Well, he's not wrong about that – we've gone deep

8

into the alley now, and reached a dismal crossroads. Looking back, I can barely make out the glow of the streetlights and traffic behind me. Down the other three ways I can see nothing at all, and it's unnaturally quiet for the centre of London. I put my hand in my pocket and pull out the thing that I've brought here.

It's a scrunched-up plastic bag.

'I still don't get how she does this,' I say, 'but here goes nothing…'

I bunch the opening of the bag in my fist and blow it up like a balloon with one long puff. As I do so, I breathe my name into the bag, almost coughing up my tonsils in the process. Then I knot the inflated bag to keep it closed, place it on the floor at the exact centre of the junction, and step back.

Nothing happens.

'Alas, she is not to be found today.' says Si, far too quickly. 'Let us be away…'

I raise my hand to stop him. There is the faintest of rustlings in the velvety silence. Before our eyes, the bag is being nudged by the ghost of a breeze, even though the air around me feels still as the grave.

'Ssh, Si. Look!'

The bag is moving now, tumbling slowly towards one of the alleyways. Then a contrary wind nudges

9

it into the air, spinning it back the way it came. Soon it's being tossed here and there, moving higher and higher, but always staying roughly above the place I put it. Yet still not a single breeze has reached me and Si. The bag rises further and further, and then...

ZZ ZiiP!

... it flashes away down the passage ahead of me, vanishing into the darkness as if caught in a hurricane.

Everything is still again.

Then I hear a creak from the alleyway ahead.

This creak is followed by another, and then another. A few tendrils of greenish mist creep towards us, and I see something moving in the shadows. The creaking grows, setting my teeth on edge, and there's a whispering, heaving sound. I step back – I can't help it – and Si whimpers, his mouth pursed tighter than a cat's bottom.

'DAN DYER...' shrieks a voice like the cry of a monstrous crow.

The first thing I see is a rusted, four-wheeled contraption, bulging and teetering with knotted bundles of plastic bags. It's a pram. Then, in a cloud of flies and baggy rustlings, an enormous gap-toothed woman with wild silver hair steps into the little winter light at the centre of the crossroads. Her eyes seem to gather that light into two dazzling points that bore right into me.

'... hello, deary!' she cries. 'Have need of old Mrs Binns, have we? You remembered the call. I always said you were a bright boy.'

'Er... hello, Mrs Binns,' I manage to say. 'Long time, no see.'

'Too long!' she shrieks in reply. 'But I've been hearing about you, Danny boy – hearing the whisper of your doings in the bags. The business with the magician – I could have helped you there. And as for that palaver in Paris...'

'How do you know about that?' I say, before I remember not to.

'Oh, I know it *all*, Dan, deary.'

Mrs Binns narrows her eyes, and puts her hands on her hips with a riot of plasticky rustlings. Over her ragged clothes, she wears loops and loops of tied-up empty shopping bags, with more stuffed under a piece of string around her waist. On one foot she wears a lady's shoe, on the other a turquoise wellington boot.

'And I know that Mr La-di-da here' – she points at Si – 'keeps you away. He dun't like me, he dun't.'

'Madam!' Si puffs, and tries to look dignified. 'I assure you, I do no such thing.'

'Scared I'll tell you more about him than he wants you to know.'

'Madam…'

'Scared you'll find out what he's been keeping from you all these years…'

'No!' Simon shouts. 'I beseech you, say nothing to the boy!'

'Huh?' I say, turning to him. 'Si, what's she talking about?'

Simon doesn't look my way. He just stares at the old woman imploringly.

'Ah, I dare say he'll tell you in his own precious time.' Mrs Binns dismisses Si with a wave of her chubby hand. 'Anyway, that's not why you came here today.'

'Er…' I already feel I've lost control of this conversation.

'Nah, you want to know about the little poltygeist that's got 'em all in a flap up at that there funny new building.'

'Er… yeah.' I say. 'At the Shard. I've never dealt with a poltergeist before.'

'And you wonder if you can deal with one now?'

I shrug. That's about the size of it. As usual, Mrs Binns is doing all the asking, as well as the answering.

'There is a disturbance in the winds,' says Mrs Binns, pulling an empty bag from her string belt and releasing it above her head with a flourish. It sweeps and tumbles in the frosty breeze, and Mrs Binns watches it intently, like an ancient soothsayer following the path of a swallow. 'The dead are getting restless. Something is disturbing them, something that's happening in *that place*.' And she points towards the sky above the passageway behind her. I follow her finger.

In the distance, I see the triangular peak of the Shard – London's greatest skyscraper – glowing in the night. As if on cue, the flying bag sweeps off towards it and vanishes from sight.

'What should I do, Mrs Binns?' I say.

Mrs Binns looks at me and chuckles darkly. She pushes the pram toward me with an ominous creak.

'Even the fullest bag is just a bag till you peek at what's inside. Take one, deary. Maybe you'll find what you're looking for.'

I glance at Si and he glances at me. Then we both turn to the mass of greasy carrier bags in the pram, which is now right under my nose. The buzzing of the bluebottle flies is repulsive, but not as much as the seething maggots and speckled brown slugs amongst the bags themselves. The old woman's grin hardens.

'Choose!' she hisses. 'And let Dame Fortune guide your hand.'

I push my purple shades up my nose. I wonder if not choosing a stinky old bag counts as a valid choice, but somehow I know it doesn't. Si is shaking his head, but it's too late for that now.

I plunge my arm into the rotten, stinking mass.

Clammy.

Cold and clammy, and wriggling.

I force myself to move my hand about, and try not to retch at the smell that rises up to me. Something scuttles over my wrist.

And up my sleeve!

I close my fingers over a loop of plastic and pull. For a moment my arm stays where it is, and I feel panic. I pull back harder, struggling, pushing at the pram with my foot. With a sucking, slathering, smacking sound I think I will never forget, my arm comes free. At the end of my dripping sleeve, a maggoty old shopping bag hangs from my fist.

'Have you chosen the bag?' breathes the voice of Mrs Binns, and I force my eyes back onto her.

Already she is receding into the winter dark of the alleyway she came from. The wheels of her pram creak as she pulls it with her. 'Or has the bag chosen you?'

'Mrs Binns!' I can't help shouting. 'What does it mean? What should I do?'

'Look in-si-d-e...' comes her voice on the wind. '... i-n-s-i-d-e... t-h-e b-a-a-a-g...'

But she is already gone.

Was she even there? I look at the bag in my hand, and for a moment it feels as if I just wandered down this back alley and picked up someone's stray piece of litter. But the look of terror on Si's face says it all.

What else can I do?

I open the bag.

2

THE WINDOW OF WONDERS

'Si, what was that about you keeping something from me?'

We arrive back at my house, Simon and me, having walked home in silence. Well, I can hardly have a conversation with a ghost only I can see as I stroll through the streets of London, can I? But now we're home – and my parents are out – I want some answers.

'It would be better if you forgot what Mrs Binns

said about that.' Si is looking evasive. 'She is an elderly person, given to fanciful ideas and no doubt bad indigestion…'

'Oh, come off it, Si! You were desperate for her not to tell me something. So, what is it?'

Si swoops about the living room, looking distressed. He seems to be wrestling with some great indecision. Then he drifts to a stop in front of the television.

'You remember the first time we met, Daniel?'

I nod. How could I forget? It was a few years ago now, and I was in a pretty dark place back then. Well, you would be too if you could see dead people and everyone thought you were mad. Si was the one who helped me get over that, put me back on my feet and got my head straight. He's been looking out for me ever since, and helping me to help those ghosts too. I owe Simon more than I like to admit.

'Yeah, I remember.'

'And when we first started helping the spirits of the dead to reach the Hereafter, you asked me a question. Do you remember that too?'

'Er… I think I asked if I could help you as well. Yeah, now I remember. I couldn't understand why you didn't want to reach the Hereafter yourself. You flapped your arms a lot and changed the subject. You do that a lot.'

Si gives an apologetic bow.

'In truth,' he says, 'there is something keeping me here, something I need to do. I just can't tell you what it is yet.'

'But why not?'

'Please don't ask me that, Daniel. I will tell you one day, that I can promise. But this is not that day.'

'Si...'

'No, Daniel. I apologise, but that is my final word on the matter.'

And he bows again.

I sigh and give up asking. It's been a long day, and I'm not in the mood for more riddles, not when I haven't even solved the mystery of Mrs Binns and her bags yet. I almost wish I hadn't bothered going to her now. I walk into the kitchen to wash the stink off my hands.

'Shall we get back to our main problem?' says Si, following me. 'The poltergeist?'

'Yeah, that,' I say. 'Thing is, Si, maybe it shouldn't be our problem at all. I mean, no one has actually asked for our help with it, have they? We wouldn't know about it at all if the ghosts we meet didn't keep going on about it.'

'Daniel, every ghost we've met in the last two weeks has mentioned the poltergeist.' Si looks serious. 'It's disturbing even the most restful spirits. Something big is going on. And you read about it on the netweb...'

'On the internet, yeah.' I correct him. Si still has trouble getting his twenty-first century lingo right. 'Even the living have noticed. But when I tried to go to the Shard to see for myself, I couldn't get in. It's been closed to casual visitors. That's why I went to Mrs Binns, to try to find out more. But all I got is a smelly old bag.'

'In truth, she does reek a bit...'

'No, Si – *this* smelly old bag.'

And I point to where I dumped the carrier bag on the floor when I came in. I can smell its fishy stink from here.

'And what was inside?' says Si, raising a solicitous eyebrow. 'You didn't actually show me.'

I glare back at him. I wonder about not telling him – that'd serve him right for holding out on me. Actually, though, I'm mostly just worried he'll laugh at me for putting my trust in a mad old bin lady when he sees what's inside. But I know I have to tell him. We're a team, after all. I tip up the bag with my foot and the object slides out.

'Oh,' Si stares down at it. 'And what is that?'

'This,' I say, picking it up, 'is a copy of *Wow TV*. It's a magazine that tells you what's on radio and TV...'

'The window of wonders!' Si gasps with delight.

'*TV*,' I correct him. 'Television. That was all that was in the bag – a tatty old magazine.' I stump off back to the living room before he can start laughing at me, and plonk myself down in my dad's favourite armchair.

'Then I was right,' Si says in his most annoying told-you-so voice as he swoops in behind me. 'We should never have gone to that Binns woman.'

I ignore him, and look at the copy of *Wow TV* in my hands. It's fourteen years out of date and looks like it spent some of that time being a tramp's pillow. An old TV guide. What can it mean?

I see the remote control for the telly on the coffee table beside me. I'm just about to look at the magazine again when my eyes fix on the remote control. It's wrapped in plastic – an annoying thing my dad does to keep dust and crumbs out of all the remotes. But it's not just any plastic. It's an old transparent supermarket carrier bag.

The kind Mrs Binns loves so much.

I pick up the remote and turn on the TV.

On the screen the face of a man with a black goatee beard appears. He has a tall, wrinkled forehead and he looks out at us above his hands. His fingers are steepled together like a church roof, and he raises one eyebrow as if daring the viewer to challenge his superior intelligence. It's not a very nice face.

'Who is that?' says Si, his eyes goggling as they always do when the TV is on. He's obsessed with it.

'I'm surprised you don't recognise him.' I say. 'That's Venn Specter. The "famous TV Psychic".'

Can you hear the sarcasm in my voice? Good.

As we watch, the opening title sequence of Venn's show rolls across the screen. We see Venn Specter stalking through a spooky old house in his stupid bottle-green polo-neck jumper, detecting psychic phenomena and solving cheesy mysteries. He's wearing his trademark jade ring pendant. He claims that when he looks through the ring – which he found in an ancient Chinese tomb – he can see ghosts.

What a fake! I've seen enough of Venn Specter to know he's just a clever fraud, fuelling his own desire for fame and fortune with the grief and credulity of others. I raise the remote to turn over.

But then I'm wondering.

Venn Specter Investigates is one of the most popular TV shows on at the moment. Is it just coincidence that it happened to be on right now? Or is Mrs Binns trying to tell me something? Despite everything, I stay on the channel and force myself to listen to Venn as he opens his terrible show.

'Good evening, ladies and gentlemen...' he says, looking over his fingertips again, '... and ghosts!'

The audience cheers and applauds. I grind my teeth.

'Tonight you join us live in central London, where I have detected a powerful distortion in the karmic web of life and death.'

I'm groaning now. The what? Give me a break.

'Stay tuned as I investigate another mystery of the supernatural...'

I roll my eyes, and point the remote to switch this rubbish off.

'... at that most iconic of skyscrapers – the Shard!'

I nearly drop the remote. I swear my purple specs almost spring off my nose.

'The Shard!' Si and I say at the same time.

'But first, let us go to a member of the audience, to see how I may be of assistance this chill December night...'

Venn drones on, taking a camera crew with him as he steps down to be with the people who have gathered to watch him. He holds out his hands and they reach to touch his fingertips. This is another of his trademarks – giving comforting messages from beyond the grave. It's not long before he's latched onto a tearful grey-haired lady who is clutching an old man's flat cap in her hands. Any fool can guess that she's just lost her husband, but Venn makes the deduction seem like a miracle. But I'm too excited to be disgusted. I raise the remote and press 'mute'.

'*This* is what Mrs Binns wanted me to see.' I jump to my feet. 'Even Venn Specter has heard of the poltergeist. He'll be taking some of his audience along with him, Si – that's how we'll get into the Shard.'

'But... but...' Si starts flapping, obviously torn between not wanting to admit that I might have been right about Mrs Binns after all, and wanting to see a real live TV show being made.

'Keep your "but" to yourself,' I say, as I pull my leather trenchcoat back on. 'Si, we need to get down there. We need to get down there now!'

3

VENN SPECTER INVESTIGATES

'You again?'

The security guard at the revolving doors of the Shard looks down and screws his brow at me. I look back at him through my trademark purple specs. Most of the rest of my face is hidden behind an enormous woolly scarf – it's blinkin' freezing, after all – so I'm surprised he recognises me.

'I told you last time,' the guard rumbles, 'the building has been closed for...'

'For routine maintenance, yeah.' I finish the sentence for him. Then I lean in and raise my eyebrow. 'But I think we both know that isn't true.'

'Don't get smart with me, kid.'

I sink into shadow as the guard looms over me.

'Okay, okay,' I say, holding my hands up. 'I doubt anyone would ever get smart with you.'

And then I slide back into the crowd before he can work out whether or not to be offended. There's no point trying to get in that way, anyway – I've already tried. Besides, I'm here for Venn Specter and his TV spectacle.

The columned space in front of the main entrance to the Shard is packed with gawpers, cameraphone jockeys and fans of Venn. Everyone is muffled up to the nostrils against the cold, but the lights of a DazzleTV film crew throw some welcome warmth down onto us. I glance at Si, and see that he's staring straight up, his mouth hanging open. I don't blame him. Above us, the great glass tower of the Shard rises high into the winter sky, blazing with light.

'Pretty cool, huh?' I whisper.

''Tis folly to build so tall,' says Si, shaking his head. 'Folly! This is not a building, Daniel, but a monstrous great crystal monument to the pride of man.'

I roll my purple eyes – I'm not in the mood for one of Si's lectures – and push my way into the crowd.

Beside a gaudy Christmas tree, a group of people in Charles Dickens get-up are singing Christmas carols, but no one's interested in them, not while Venn Specter is communing with the spirit world on live TV. I push in further, trying to get near the front. And then I see him, bottle-green pullover and everything.

'I feel a message coming through,' Venn cries, waving his arms like they're his psychic antennae or something. 'Someone from the other side wants to get in touch. It's a message from beyond the grave!'

The audience holds its breath, everyone glancing at everyone else to see who will react. Venn darts about, holding his hands out toward people, tuning in. I'm at the front now, and for a moment he looks straight at me, but one glimpse of my raised eyebrow and purple specs is enough for him, it seems, and he passes on.

'What's he doing?' says Si, floating right above me in a ghastly cloud of ectoplasm. If Venn Specter was even half the psychic he claims to be, he'd be all over Si like a rash. But it's clear he can't see my right-hand spook any more than anyone else can.

'They call this "cold reading",' I mumble in my scarf to Si, hoping no-one notices me apparently talking to myself. 'He's searching for clues in the way people look and behave. Then, if he guesses something right, he can pretend a ghost told him.'

Si scowls. 'So he really is nothing but a cheap fraud?'

'You bet. And since it's those who've lost loved ones who are most attracted to Venn's shows, he won't have long to look.'

Sure enough, Venn Specter's hands come to rest pointing at a little girl.

'Oh, poor sweet child!' Venn says, hamming it up. 'Your darling little heart has been broken. Has someone dear to you passed away?'

The little girl – who wears a glitzy plastic tiara and a princess dress under her coat – can't be much more than four years old. She wipes a green bogey from her nose and sniffs, her eyes as big as oceans. The crowd gives a collective gasp of concern. A woman, who must be the little girl's mum, nudges her and says, 'Go on, Stacey. Tell the nice man.'

'Yes,' blubs Venn, pursing his lips like he's talking to a baby. 'Tell me who you have lost, dear, sweet little girl.'

'It's my Pop,' says the girl, sniffing again, and looking close to tears. 'But he's not lost. Pop's dead.'

Venn turns to the crowd.

'The little girl has lost her pop! Her father has died!'

The crowd gasps and sighs. Women clasp their gloved hands to their bosoms. A DazzleTV cameraman zooms in so close to the little girl's face, that he's in danger of getting snot on the lens.

Venn, clearly seeing the chance to dial up the emotional tone a point or two, crouches down beside the girl, so that they can both be in camera shot.

'Poor Stacey.' He wipes a fake tear from his eye. 'It must be so hard. Tell us about your pop.'

'Well,' says Stacey in a small voice. 'He did good cuddles…'

The crowd goes 'Aaaaw!'

'… and he was very hairy,' Stacey adds, with a sniff.

Venn blinks, and seems briefly at a loss to know what to say, but he recovers quickly.

'Ah, he had a beard, did he, your pop?'

'Yes,' says Stacey, her bottom lip trembling. 'Pop had a wuvely fuzzy chin.'

Well, the crowd and the film crew can't get

enough of this, can they? I even hear the cameraman say something about 'televisual gold!' to one of his colleagues. Venn knows he has everyone's attention now, and starts giving poor little Stacey a heart-warming message from her dead father.

Now, ordinarily I'd be disgusted by this – Venn Specter should be thoroughly ashamed of himself – but I've just noticed something. Something no-one else can see except me.

There's another ghost here.

A ghost that's keeping very close to little Stacey. Or rather, close to Stacey's feet. And believe me, it's not the girl's dad. I point it out to Si as discreetly as I can.

'But what is that?' says Si, squinting down. 'It looks like a rat.'

'Not a rat, Si,' I say. 'It's a hamster.'

And it really is. A little furry, ectoplasmic hamster ghost, snuggling up to the girl's twinkly shoes.

'That,' I whisper to Si, 'must be Pop.'

'But…' Si clearly needs to think about this. 'I don't understand.'

'Oh, come on, Si!' I hiss. 'The hairyness, the cuddles, the "wuvely fuzzy chin". Pop isn't Stacey's dad – "Pop" is the name of her pet!'

Si's eyes go wide. One look at Stacey's mum's face is enough to show I'm right. She looks completely confused by what's happening, but at the same time, she's obviously too shy to challenge the star of Venn Specter Investigates while the cameras are rolling.

But shyness has never been my problem. Behind the scarf, an enormous grin spreads across my face. Suddenly I see a way to make Venn Specter look like a complete dufus, and on national TV too.

'I'm going to enjoy this,' I say.

'Wait, Daniel…' Si starts to protest, but I tune him out. He's probably going to remind me why we're really here, but I just can't resist it. Venn Specter feeds on other people's grief like a parasite. But not tonight. Tonight I'm going to serve him up a very public slice of humble pie.

'Can you really see the ghost of this girl's dad?' I shout out to Venn, making everyone turn to face me. The cameras spin my way too.

'Why, yes,' says Venn, looking not too pleased at being interrupted. 'And I was just passing on his message of hope to poor little Stacey here, so if you don't mind…'

'But I'd like to know,' I go on regardless, as

everyone watches me, 'did Stacey's Pop like going round in his little wheel?'

'Oh, yes!' squeals Stacey. 'He went round and round!'

'And did your Pop like to hide in the straw at the bottom of his cage?'

'Yes, oh yes!' Stacy is jumping up and down now. 'He always did his poos in the straw. Naughty Pop and his poppy poop!'

Confused laughter ripples round the crowd. Everyone is staring at me, then at Stacey, then at Venn. Venn Specter goes suddenly pale as he realises he's made some error. He gives me a furious look, and gets ready to launch a desperate bid to save the situation, but I call out again before he can.

'So Pop isn't your dad at all, is he, Stacey?' I say. 'He's your pet hamster.'

'Yes, my little fuzzy hamster.' Stacey's face lights up. Then it falls. 'I miss my Pop. My little Popsy!'

She sits down on the pavement and bursts into tears.

Some of the audience are laughing out loud now. Other people are staring in disbelief at Stacey. Some are even looking imploringly at Venn, apparently waiting for him to explain how he can make such a terrible mistake. And me? Well, I'm still grinning from ear to ear. Venn Specter's made a right chump of himself this time, hasn't he?

Then I catch the look of ice-cold hatred on Specter's face, and the grin slips a bit. I look to the TV crew for support but they turn their backs on me, taking the camera off into the crowds. I see Venn click his fingers. A shadow looms behind me, and a hand the size of a gorilla's paw lands on my shoulder.

4

THE CAMERA NEVER LIES
(IT DOESN'T NEED TO)

The next thing I know I'm being escorted – politely, but firmly – to a small bus with a DazzleTV logo on the side. Considering I've just been the centre of everyone's attention, it's shocking how quickly the crowd have turned away from me. But the eyes of the crowd are on Venn again, as he hastily changes the subject back to the mystery of the Shard poltergeist.

The man who is nearly crushing my shoulder with his beefy hand is enormous. A name tag on his lapel says simply 'Ned'. He pushes me through the door of the bus, and I find myself in the glitzy, slightly stinky mobile dressing room of Venn Specter.

'Make yourself at home, sir,' says Ned, with an American drawl and the cool eye of an ex-soldier. 'Mr Specter will be along in a moment.'

I raise my finger to say something witty and devastating, but he slams the door in my face. Which is probably just as well.

'Daniel?' says Si, swooshing in through the door, and coming to my side. 'Are you all right?'

'Yeah,' I say, rearranging my lapels. 'Just a bit confused. Didn't those people see what happened? Venn dropped a clanger, but they're still out there listening to him.'

'I'm afraid you are forgetting the power of belief, Daniel. These people want to believe in Venn Specter. More than they want to believe in you.'

'But he got it wrong!'

'For a moment, yes,' says Si, with his best gothic butler's expression. 'But alas, he has already won the crowd back. I fear that you have done nothing but draw attention to yourself, Daniel.'

I snort, and push my hands into my pockets, searching for something to say. But I've got a horrible feeling Si's right, as usual. And after what I've just done, will Venn let me follow him into the Shard as we'd hoped? The look on Si's face says it all.

Ah, crapsticks.

The door of the bus bursts open, and Venn Specter storms in. Ned, the polite gorilla, pulls the door shut behind them. The inside of the bus seems to shrink as the two men loom at me.

'Name?' snaps Venn.

'Er…' I say. 'Well, you're Venn Specter, and he's Ned…'

'Your name, wise guy!' Venn blazes at me.

I gulp, and tell them.

'Now then, *Dan*, I've just checked with the girl's mother. You have no connection with the family at all, so how in hell's name did you know about the hamster?'

I open my mouth to speak. Then I shut it again. I haven't quite thought this bit through.

'Um…' I say at last. 'Lucky guess?'

Venn grinds his teeth and tugs his goatee.

'Too lucky! Now I've got to get back out there and work this crowd again, thanks to you. And then

I've got to get into this stupid great building and give them a poltergeist they'll never forget, or my ratings will slide.' He leans over me till his hooked nose is almost touching mine. 'And I don't like it when my ratings slide. I don't like it at all. It makes me...' more grinding of teeth '... *cross.*'

And he gives me a little shove with his forefinger that sends me staggering back.

The atmosphere's pretty nasty in the bus now. Probably I should shut up and keep my head down, but this just isn't fair. He's the one who should be trembling, not me. He's the bad guy, after all. I set my specs.

'You don't scare me,' I say, and I hope it sounds like I mean it. 'You lie to people when they're sad and vulnerable. You deserve to be found out for what you are: a lousy, low-down conman, with a black conscience and a... a... bad taste in pullovers.'

Veins bulge on Venn's forehead and he goes bright red.

'Proud of that little speech, are you?' he snarls. 'You're better than me, I suppose. You think that your "sad and vulnerable" people want the truth? I give them hope! I give them comfort when they are lost in despair. What would you give them? Hamsters? And

37

the cold hard truth that there is *nothing* after death, *nothing at all?* You think they'd rather hear that?'

I glance at Si, and he glances back. Venn's wrong about death, about as wrong as he can be. But it's hard to avoid the thought that he might – just might – have a teeny tiny point about the other stuff. I find I don't know what to say.

'Now, I need to get into the Shard,' Venn continues, mastering his temper. 'And I need to take someone from the audience with me, because those dimwit TV people think it's good for the show. So cancel your plans, Danny Boy, because I've got a poltergeist to bust and you're coming with me.'

'What?' I can hardly believe my ears.

'You heard. There's something about this hamster business that I need to work out. Until I have, I'm keeping you firmly in my sights.'

There's a knock on the door, and Ned opens it. A woman with a clipboard pops her head in, and says, 'Everything okay, Venn? Did the boy agree?'

'Oh yes, he's agreed all right,' says Venn Specter before I can say anything. 'But I'm only taking him. No one else.'

'No can do, I'm afraid,' says the woman. 'The producer wants you to take the little girl.'

'What?' Venn looks appalled.

'She's perfect,' says the woman. 'So sweet and telegenic, and the audience adore her. And you need to get the live audience back on-side after what just happened.' She gives me a disapproving look.

Venn grinds his teeth yet again, but there's nothing he can do. Then the bus gets even more crowded as little Stacey and her mother are led in.

I look at the mother, and wonder if common sense will prevail and make her take her daughter away from all this madness. But one glance at her star-struck expression, and I see it's no good. I bet she's already dreaming of Stacey becoming a film star. Someone from Makeup comes in and starts powdering my nose. Stacey's nose needs a good wipe with a tissue first.

I look down at the little girl, and find she's staring up at me. I try a grin, and waggle my fingers at her. I can deal with ghosts and ghouls and the undead, but little girls dressed up as princesses are way beyond my experience. Then I notice that the scrawny spirit of Pop the hamster is still snuffling about at her feet.

'Hey, I'm sorry about Pop,' I say to Stacey, crouching down so that our eyes are level.

She gives me a brave sniff.

'But I'm glad you had the time with him that you did.'

I reach down to Pop, and put my hand on him gently. I know he won't be able to feel me – he's just a ghost, after all – but he sees my hand and tries to snuggle up to it. I make an action as if stroking him. He gives a single spectral squeak of pleasure, rolls over onto his back, and vanishes in a puff of golden ectoplasm.

That's all he wanted, you see – one last stroke. And now he's gone, off to whatever part of the Hereafter has been reserved for small fuzzy rodents.

Stacey gives me a funny look. I wink at her, and stand up again. I promise myself there and then that whatever insanity is about to happen to us, I won't let any of it impact on Stacey.

Then the TV people lead us out of the bus to the waiting crowd.

5

TELEVISUAL GOLD

We're a funny little group as we're led through the cheering crowd toward the top of a downward escalator. Venn in the lead, all goatee beard and mystery; me behind trying to hide behind my lapels; Stacy holding her mum's hand; and then Ned. I try to spot signs that the crowd might have lost some of its faith in Venn Specter, but it's almost as if my little exposé of earlier never happened. I glance at Si, and he shrugs as if to say 'People, eh?' or 'What did you expect?'

Venn begins talking to the crowd – and the lens of a huge TV camera – explaining that we will now be entering the 'zone of poltergeist activity', and that as few people as possible will be permitted, so as not to 'disturb the ghostly essences' and blah-di-blah.

As he speaks, some technicians come forward and start strapping a power-pack onto Ned's back. Then they give him a surprisingly small camera that looks ridiculous as they mount it on a bracket that he braces on his vast shoulder. It's obvious he's going to be the only film crew for this moment of television madness. By the calm look on his face, I'd say this is how all Venn Specter's investigations are filmed.

Then, with a flourish, Venn turns and wishes his audience goodbye. He leads us down the escalator. Behind us, the crowd lean over the railing to watch us descend. As I look back I see for the first time that a huge TV screen is hanging from a neighbouring building. The image on it changes as Ned's camera comes on-line, showing a Ned's-eye view of the situation. In this way, the audience will be able to see everything that happens to us in the Shard. Right now, though, the only thing on the screen is a giant close-up of my startled face. I look back at Ned and find he's staring right at me. I can't help noticing his free hand is a fist of knuckles.

'To begin this investigation, we will enter the famous Shard through the public entrance,' Venn says to Ned's camera, shoving me out of the way. 'From there we will ride the elevators to the very summit of the building, to the spectacular viewing platform. But first, we will meet a member of staff who has a strange story to tell.'

We reach the bottom of the escalator where a woman in a Shard uniform leads us into the building. At the end of a corridor, we find ourselves at the gleaming ticket desks and gift shop. The place is dimly lit, and I wonder why. Surely not just to create a spooky ambience for TV. A quick scope of the place shows there are no ghosts lurking here. There is a gaggle of staff waiting near the ticket counters though. Venn leads us straight to them.

'Greetings,' he says, with a cheesy bow. 'My name is Venn Specter and I am here to investigate. Which one of you is…' He discreetly checks a card in his hand. '… Tim?'

'That's me,' says a short man in a Shard uniform who doesn't know what to do with his hands. Those

43

hands, as well as his face, are covered in dozens of little pieces of skin-coloured sticking plaster.

'Ah, Tim,' Venn croons. 'They say you have witnessed a strange and terrible thing. They say you have seen...' Venn pauses for effect. '... the poltergeist.'

Tim jumps at this, and looks even more like a rabbit staring at approaching headlights.

'I... I... yes,' he manages to say. 'I saw it. At least, not it. No one can see a poltergeist. I saw what it can do.'

'Aaaah!' Venn sighs with satisfaction, motioning Ned to zoom in a bit on Tim's face. 'Do tell us what happened, Tim.'

'Er, well, I was here at night, just as we were closing up the shop...'

'A night like this?' Venn butts in. 'At around the same time we're here now?'

Tim gives a little squeak of fright and nods.

'Ah, good,' says Venn. 'Proceed.'

Tim gulps. 'I was just straightening up the postcards and guide books and that, when I... well, when I felt a tap on my shoulder.'

'Yes?' Venn leans in even closer, his teeth yellow-white above his goatee beard as he leers at Tim.

'Well, I turned round and I saw, I saw…' Tim dries up, as white as the back of a postcard himself now.

'Yesss?' Venn hisses, like he's about to explode. 'What did you see?'

'A… a… a pencil!' Tim's hands jump to his mouth. 'A pencil *floating in the air!* Flying on its own! It jabbed me again and again and again. There was blood on my face. I grabbed it, but then… then the whole display of gift shop pencils just exploded! There were hundreds of them, all flying at me. Stabbing and stabbing and…'

Tim breaks down in sobs. Venn rolls his eyes, but indicates for Ned to keep the camera on the blubbing man.

I dig a packet of tissues out of my pocket and give one to Tim. Then, before Venn can stop me, I ask Tim a question of my own.

'When this happened, yeah?' I say. 'Had you been doing or saying something that might have provoked an attack?'

Tim blinks at me.

'No,' he says. 'I was just doing what my supervisor told me to do. Which was tidy up.'

Something about the angry way Tim says 'supervisor' makes me want to press him on this, but before I can ask any anything else, Venn whispers in my ear. 'Zip it, kid! Get your own TV show.'

Venn is just about to go back to his own numbskull line of questioning, when Tim's head snaps up.

'What's that?' he says. 'Did you hear it? I heard a sound.'

Well, actually I *did* hear something – a clattering sound from deep in the shadows of the darkened shop. We all go quiet, and Ned starts to pan the camera around slowly. There is nothing there, only shadows and darkness.

'Ladies and gentlemen,' says Venn in a dramatic whisper. 'Something is happening. We are not alone. Come, follow me as I investigate further.' Then he puts the jade ring pendant to his eye – the one he claims lets him see ghosts – and begins to creep forward like an intrepid explorer into the unknown. The rest of us follow.

Normally I'd laugh at the sight, but not this time. What was it we heard? I strain my eyes into the gloom, but I swear I can't see any ghostly presences. There's no one there at all.

Tim, who creeps forward beside me, is shaking all over. I know because his torch beam is quivering all over the place. I take the torch from his hand and stroll forward, sweeping the light from side to side, ignoring Venn's hisses of protest. Well, I'm the expert in the room, aren't I? Even if I'm the only one who knows it. Then my torch beam lights up something on the floor.

It's a keyring.

The others gather round, and for a moment we all stare at it. Then Venn jumps in to make the moment as exciting as possible.

'Ned, are you getting this?' he says, snatching the torch from my hand and shining it onto the keyring like it's a rare and magical artefact. 'Dear viewers, as you can see this keyring is nearly a metre away – a whole metre! – from its rightful place in this immaculate and well ordered shop.' He swings the beam over to the very neat display of keyrings nearby. 'There is only one possible explanation. It has been moved here by ghostly forces from beyond the realm of the physical world. It has been flung here…' He pauses for dramatic effect, shining the torch up into his face. '… by the poltergeist!'

6

THE VIEW FROM THE SHARD

It takes Venn a full five minutes to finally exhaust the dramatic potential of a fallen keyring. And he's good, I'll give him that. By the time he's finished, Tim is a nervous wreck, and the rest of them are pretty spooked too. Venn wraps up the scene, gives Tim an encouraging pat on the shoulder, and asks him to lead us round to the lift.

'Why's it so dark everywhere?' I ask when we reach the gleaming doors to the elevator.

'Power problems,' Tim says, opening a security panel beside the lift with a shaking hand and inserting a key. 'It comes and goes. Been happening since... well, since all this weirdness started.'

'Power problems?' I ask. 'How are we going to use the lift if there's something wrong with the electricity?'

'We're on the emergency generator,' says Tim, as the doors slide open to reveal a mirrored interior.

'Oh.' I glance at Si. Suddenly I'm not so sure about getting into this lift.

'Is it safe?' asks Stacey's mum, pulling her daughter close.

'Yes, dear lady.' Venn steps into the lift. 'There is no danger while you are with me. Come, please do not be afraid.'

I look at Stacey's mum, half expecting this to be the moment she comes to her senses, but under the glare of the camera – and the sickly smile of Venn Specter – she just gives a shrug and steers Stacey into the lift.

'Is the weirdy boy with the funny glasses coming too?' Stacey asks her mum, pointing at me.

Everyone stares at yours truly.

Ah, this is nuts. I shove my hands in my pockets,

and get into the lift. The door slides shut, and we start to climb. But by the way my stomach is pressed down, it feels more like 'take off' than a gentle ascent – it's so fast!

'The Shard is the tallest skyscraper in Western Europe,' says Tim, who seems to have slipped into tour guide mode. 'It is 310 metres tall, and this lift travels at six metres per second. The windows are cleaned by professional mountaineers, who abseil down from the summit. We hope you enjoy your visit to the Shard today.'

Then the doors open, and we're out. But this isn't the end of the journey. The Shard is so tall, that you have to change elevators half way up. Fortunately, Tim forgets to give us any more tourist stuff as we rocket up to our final destination: the summit of the Shard.

Ping

The lift doors swish open onto a darkened corridor. The only light is from emergency strips set just above the floor.

'We have arrived.' Venn breathes the words into Ned's camera, turning the torch onto his face again. 'We must keep our wits about us. For I sense the powerful presence of a paranormal entity.'

I can't help giving a snort. The only thing I can sense is the powerful presence of Venn's cheesy lines and naff delivery. I step out of the lift first, and throw a smile to Stacey. I'm pleased to see she's apparently unfazed by Venn's attempts to scare us. Shame I can't say the same for her mother and Tim.

'Stay close to me, darling,' Stacey's mum says in a quavering voice as they follow me out.

Around a corner are some stairs up to the viewing level. I take them three at a time, eager to see what's up there. Then I skid to a stop, my mouth falling open as I come face to face with the view from the Shard.

''Tis wondrous!' gasps Si, floating up behind me, and staring out through the floor-to-ceiling windows.

And it is. London at night spreads beneath us like a carpet of gleaming jewels, divided by a ribbon of velvety black that can only be the Thames. The lit dome of St Paul's Cathedral shines silver-white, amidst tiny stacks of bright office windows. I see the pods of the London Eye like gleaming pearls on a necklace. I see the distant face of Big Ben like a pocket watch of gold. The red and white sparkle of traffic flows throughout it all.

'Ooh, pretty!' says Stacey, as the others arrive beside me.

'It is, sweetheart,' says her mum, and even Venn stops yabbering for a moment to goggle at the sight of London glittering in the night.

'Nearly as pretty as the pretty lady,' says Stacey.

There's a long pause. I think we're all so amazed by the view that we don't realise at first what Stacey has just said.

'What pretty lady?' says her mum.

'That one,' Stacey says, pointing into the dark behind us. The air is suddenly freezing.

We all turn where we stand.

Slowly.

Even I feel the hairs on the back of my neck stand up when we see that no one's there.

'Oh, she's gone now,' says Stacey. 'Pretty lady? Pretty lady, come back!'

She starts to run to the stairs, but her mother grabs her. Tim makes a whimpering sound and clutches Ned's arm. I raise my eyebrow at Si.

'I saw nothing,' he says. 'But there is… something here. Can you sense it, Daniel?'

I nod. I don't want to start speaking out loud to my invisible sidekick, not with Stacey and her mum there, and Tim close to wetting himself. But I want Si to know that, yes, I can sense something:

that faint fizzing crackle in the air when a ghost is close.

Venn raises his jade ring to his eye and begins to prowl around the viewing platform, keeping a constant running commentary going for Ned and his camera. Goodness only knows what the audience down below in the street are making of Ned's live feed to the big screen. Not to mention the rest of the nation, glued to their not-so-big screens at home.

I wonder about asking Stacey to tell me exactly what she saw, but her mother is clutching her so close that I decide not to push it. Instead I turn to Tim.

'Down below, when I asked you if you'd done or said anything to provoke an attack, yeah?' I try to sound business-like and reassuring. 'You said something about your supervisor. It sounded like you don't like her very much.'

Tim gives me a startled look, then glances at Ned. I guess he's making sure the camera's mic is out of range.

'My supervisor's a proper tyrant.' Tim's whispering, but he seems pleased to steer the conversation back to everyday things. 'She's always bossing everyone around. No one likes her. Why do you want to know?'

'Well, I'm just wondering if you said anything to her when she told you to tidy up. Not to her face maybe, but perhaps you muttered something under your breath?'

Tim gives a nervous smile.

'Yeah, I might've done. Don't ask me what though. She's a right nasty old witch, that one.'

There's a sudden, deafening sound…

PANG!

… that drowns out Tim's words. Across the window pane beside us a razor thin fracture has appeared, reaching from one side of the viewing platform to the other.

Venn comes running back.

'The window's broken!' he says into the camera. 'Are you getting this, Ned? The window's cracked from side to side!'

'Could it be a bird?' Stacey's mum's voice is a tiny frightened squeak. 'A pigeon flying into the window?'

'No way,' says Tim. 'Even if you fired a hundred pigeons from a cannon, they wouldn't crack this glass. It's virtually bullet proof!'

A new sound reaches us now, on an icy breeze. It's

like some great frost giant has just breathed out over us, with a dismal moaning sigh.

'You must be able to hear that!' Venn says into the camera. 'Ladies and gentlemen, something is happening in the Shard. Listen!'

The wind grows stronger, its moan growing deeper and yet more human.

'We need to get out of here,' I say, steering Stacey's mum, with Stacey clinging to her coat, toward the stairs back down to the lift. Tim is already running that way with his hands over his head as if the sky is about to fall on him. I look back and see Venn hesitate, his eyes wild. I get the feeling he's struggling to keep up his TV persona in the face of some genuinely spooky stuff.

'We shall... withdraw.' He shouts into the camera, above the roaring wind. 'To assess these... extraordinary events, which... which...'

The wind grows louder, reaching a sudden shrieking crescendo. Venn Specter gives up and runs, terrified, down the stairs...

...just as the window explodes inwards behind him.

Chunks of glass the size of ice cubes rattle down the stairs around us, as the winter wind roars into the viewing platform in a blizzard of snow. We stagger to the lift, Tim scrabbling to get the key in the panel. The lift doors slide open with a *ping*, and we pile in.

'Are you getting this?' Venn gasps at Ned.

The big man turns the camera round, sees that the red light is still on, and gives a quick nod. Tim jabs the buttons of the lift, and the doors start to close.

Then they stop.

Stacey's mum has jammed her foot between them.

'Where's Stacey?' she cries. 'Oh my God, I've lost Stacey!'

We look about us. It's true – the little girl isn't in the lift. I jump back out into the corridor again. And that's when I hear something from back up the stairs. A little voice carrying down to us on the bitter wind.

'Pretty lady,' says Stacey. 'I wish I could be pretty like you.'

Stacey's mum screams.

I rush toward the stairs, to where Stacey must be. But I don't even reach the first step before I'm lifted clean off my feet by an icy blast that flips me over and drives the breath from my body. I crash back down in the doorway of the lift. I try to stand again, but a second gust propels me further back, pinning me and the others to the back wall of the lift. We can only watch in horror as the doors slide shut.

Ping

Then the lift is falling. And no, I'm not exaggerating – I really do mean *falling!* It's like the cable has been cut or something. We all rise up off the floor, weightless for a moment as the elevator hurtles down to earth like a plummeting stone.

7

GOING DOWN...

I just have time to think two thoughts:

1. Woo, I'm weightless! I've always wanted to know what that feels like. :-)
2. Shame I'll be dead in, like, one second flat though. And I do mean flat. :-O

Then I'm tumbling to the floor of the lift again in a pile of limbs, Venn's beard, Ned's camera, Stacey's mum, and Tim. There is a terrible, screaming sound all around, and the lift is juddering, slowing all the time. At about the point I expected to be smashed into atoms, the lift rattles to a halt. It gives a final shake and then smacks the ground with a rude, bone-jarring crash.

But we're still alive.

'What on earth happened?' Venn says, staggering to his feet.

'Emergency braking.' Tim's muffled voice comes up from somewhere beneath Ned. 'The lift can't just fall... cof.'

'Did you...?' Venn turns to Ned.

'Yes, sir,' says Ned, getting to his feet and turning the camera back onto Venn as if nearly falling to your death in a runaway lift is all part of a day's work. 'Camera's still rolling.'

Ping

The lift doors slide open, and we stagger out. My legs feel like they're made of marshmallow. Si rises up through the carpet at my feet in a cloud of hazy ectoplasm, his eyes still ratting round their sockets. I guess the force of the fall sent him ghosting down through the floors below. And that reminds me we're only half way down the Shard right now –

59

at the point where we had to change lifts going up.

'Stacey!'

Stacey's mum begins to wail. She's still in the lift, jabbing at all the buttons.

'Why won't it go? I've got to go back for Stacey!'

'It's no good,' Tim explains. 'This lift is out of action now.'

'But my Stacey is all alone!'

I glance at Si and he raises an eyebrow in reply. Stacey may be a lot of things right now, but one thing she is not is alone. The real question is: who, or what, is the 'pretty lady'?

'My dear woman,' says Venn, placing his hand on Stacey's mum's shoulder, and motioning Ned to zoom in close. 'I swear to you by all that is holy, in this world and the next, that I will find your daughter.'

Stacey's mum stops hammering on the dead panel of the lift and turns a look of desperate hope on to Venn Specter.

'Bring her to me! Please, just… bring her back safe.' Then she bursts into sobs and buries her face in Venn's bottle-green polo neck sweater. Venn holds her close and turns to the camera like a hero.

'I promise you,' he declares. 'I will bring Stacey home.'

Televisual gold.

I want to be sick.

Tim leads Stacey's mum – who is blowing trumpet sounds into a fistful of paper towels – to the downward lift. For a moment it looks like he's going to try and make us join them, but in the end he just shakes his head and looks relieved when the doors close. The lift descends to safety.

I'm just straightening the lapels of my coat, when I notice that Venn is eyeing me up. He turns to Ned and makes a throat-cutting 'time out' gesture. Ned lowers the camera, the red light winking out.

'You seem remarkably calm, kid, given what just happened up there,' Venn says to me, his huge forehead furrowing.

I shrug. Well, I've been through worse, I guess.

'But I wonder what did happen,' he goes on. 'Some kind of freak wind or something. There's always a rational explanation. Not that I tell my viewers that, of course.'

I raise my eyebrows. He's being very chummy all of a sudden.

'You don't actually believe in ghosts, do you?' I say.

Venn chuckles. 'Oh, right, and you do, I suppose? Of course there's no such thing as ghosts. Only an idiot would believe in that old clap-trap.'

Clap-trap?

'What if I could *prove* to you that ghosts exists?' I say, glancing at Si. 'What if I *showed* you a ghost? What would you say then?'

Venn laughs. Darkly. The chumminess vanishes completely as he steps closer.

'Say? I wouldn't say anything, boy. I'd be too busy filming it and sticking it up on YouTube with my name in big letters. Why should I waste my time saying *anything* to a nobody like you? You just don't get it, do you, kid? Whether ghosts exist or not, I'll still come out the winner. And do you know why?'

'Er…'

Venn leans down over me. He's eaten garlic recently.

'Because I'm famous.'

Oh.

'Whereas you…' He wrinkles his nose in mock disgust. 'You're just… *ordinary*.'

'If I'm so ordinary,' I say, annoyed that this has all got so personal all of a sudden, 'how did I know about the hamster?'

Venn shrugs.

'Yes, that. Well, maybe you really did just get lucky. Frankly, kid, I'm disappointed. You know, for a moment down there I thought maybe you had seen something. But it turns out you're no more interesting than any of the other dumb schmucks who watch my show. And now I've got you away from the crowd, you can just slink back to Nowheresville where you came from, and keep your mouth shut.'

'But…' I hold up my finger.

'Leave it, kid,' he says, turning his back on me. 'You've had your fifteen minutes of fame. Now it's time for the professionals to get busy. You can take the lift back down.'

And with this, Ned raises the camera again, and Venn goes on with the show.

'Ladies and gentlemen, as you have seen, exciting and terrible events have taken place at the Shard. We have captured on film proof that a ghostly presence has taken control of the building. Not only that, it has seized an innocent little girl! But I am Venn Specter, and I am not so easily deterred. I will continue alone from here, armed with my jade ring and my long years of experience. I will uncover the secret at the heart of this affair, and save poor little Stacey from her terrible fate. So follow me, dear viewers, as I, Venn Specter, investigate further.'

And with a flourish, he turns on his heel and vanishes around a corner, Ned jogging along behind him.

'A most unpleasant individual.' Si snorts. 'Would you like me to materialise in a cloud of dust motes and terrify him to the foundations of his soul?'

'Nah,' I say. 'At least, not yet. But I'm not letting him get away from me that easily.'

I stroll off after Venn. But when I turn the corner, I stop when I see what's there.

Which is precisely nothing.

Venn and Ned have gone. It's like they've vanished into thin air.

'What trickery is this?' demands Si, at my side.

We turn around, staring at the blank walls and carpet of the corridor. Ahead there is nothing but the open door of the empty out-of-order lift.

'There must be another door here?' I say, tapping at various wall panels at random.

'But Daniel, how does Venn Specter know of secret doors?'

'He's got a whole film crew behind him, remember? He's probably studied plans of the building, and knows where all the emergency exits are. But if he thinks he can escape me, he's mistaken. I've got something he hasn't.'

'Oh, and what, pray, is that?'

'You, Si, you great numpty!' I roll my eyes. 'Now stop fiddling with your pony tail and get ghosting through these walls. We've got to find that hidden door.'

He does so, pushing his spectral head through the wall panels one by one, until he emerges with a puff of ectoplasm and a triumphant cry.

'There are stairs behind this panel,' he declares. 'You were right. There is a secret door.'

I run my fingers around the panel, and tap on it. Nothing much happens, and there's no sign that it can open at all, not even any visible hinges.

'You know, Si, despite everything, I think things have just turned out pretty good for us.'

'I admire your optimism.' Si scowls at me. 'But

we have been attacked by something we cannot identify, you have almost died falling down the lift shaft, and that poor Stacey child is in the clutches of a power unlike any we have encountered before. I hardly see…'

Si trails off when he sees me lean on the panel. When my hand presses it in just the right place, there's a click and the panel swings open.

In the flickering neon beyond we see the stairs.

'I know all that, Si,' I say. 'But at the same time, we've just got exactly what we wanted all along.'

He looks confused.

'We're in the Shard, aren't we? All alone. With no security guards, and no more cameras. And that's just how I like it.'

'Indeed we are.' Si smiles his ghastliest smile and bows his frilliest bow. He flourishes his hand towards the open door. 'Then after you, Master Dyer.'

I set my purple specs, and adjust my lapels. It's time to do what I do best. It's time to get down to business.

I stroll through the door.

8

A QUICK WORKOUT

'Is there a plan, at all?' says Si, floating at my side as I climb the stairs. It's even darker here than the corridor below, and the lights keep cutting out altogether. 'I only ask because I'm usually the last to find out.'

'Don't think we know enough yet for a plan,' I gasp between steps. 'We're still in the, er, fact-finding phase of the operation.'

I've run up several flights of stairs by now, jogged

up a few more, staggered up the rest, and now I'm almost on my hands and knees. Looking up, the stairs go on and on, spiralling into the darkness above.

'Oh, I see.' Si sounds unimpressed. 'Well, don't forget to tell me when we've found a fact, Daniel. I'm beginning to forget what one of those looks like.'

I sit down on the floor of a landing, puffed out. But not too puffed put to put Si in his place.

'Oh, come off it, Si. We've found out one fact at least.'

'And what's that?'

'That the poltergeist is the ghost of a woman,' I say. 'Unless the meaning of the phrase "pretty lady" has changed since I last looked in a dictionary.'

On the landing where I sit, a double door marked 'Fire Escape' in glowing red letters is half open. There is nothing but darkness beyond. I decide not to bother with it. Well, I've got a lot of stairs still to go, haven't I? I drag myself to my feet and put a foot on the step of the next flight of stairs going up.

A great, ringing, clamouring sound reaches me from above. I look up. It's dark, but something flashes in the emergency lighting far above. Then, as I stare, an office photocopier flies into view, brushes my shoulder and then hits the concrete floor right beside me, exploding into a hail of plastic bits and glass.

''Zooks!' Si roars, raising his hands to shine their ghostlight up the stairwell. 'Run, Daniel! Get out of the way!'

Looking up again, I just have time to see a tumbling mass of furniture, TV screens, and kitchen equipment, rushing down at me.

I dive through the fire door with a cry of 'Crapsticks!' A sound like a meteorite strike fills the air, as the falling things hit the landing where I was just standing.

I roll to a stop and look back at the doorway. The landing and stairwell are jammed solid with twisted metal and ruined stuff. It'd take hours to shift it.

And now there's another sound, too – a high, almost tinkling human sound.

Laughter.

I look at Si.

'For somebody described as a pretty lady,' he says, 'our poltergeist has a very un-ladylike approach to keeping visitors at bay.'

I nod. I wonder for a moment if Venn and Ned were caught on the stairs above, but something tells me they weren't.

'I bet Venn came this way too,' I say, getting unsteadily to my feet and brushing myself down. 'That must be why the door was open. Come on, Si – we've got to find another way up.'

We're in a large, open-plan space reaching all the way to the glass sides of the building. There are strange shapes all around me, barely visible in the emergency ceiling lights and the glow from the city outside. For a moment, in my rattled frame of mind, I think the shapes are creatures, poised to spring at me, but then the main lights come on unexpectedly. I raise my hands to my eyes against the sudden, blinding light, though just as my eyes get used to it, it cuts out again. But not before I've seen what those strange shapes are.

'Exercise machines,' I say. 'Si, we're in a gym! This must be the hotel that's in the middle of the Shard. There's even supposed to be a swimming pool up here somewhere.'

As I speak the lights come on again, but faintly this time, flickering. The gym is panelled with gleaming wood and there is a marble floor, but it's hard to focus with the dodgy lights.

'What *is* wrong with the electrics?'

'Electricity is a little after my time, Daniel,' says Si with a sniff. 'As you know, ghostly manifestations can interfere with your modern lighting. However, I've never known it affect a whole building like this.'

I cross the gym, surprised that it's so completely empty. Then I remember that apart from Tim and a few members of staff, I haven't seen anyone else in the Shard at all. I see the orange splat of a dropped smoothie congealing on the marble, beside a towel and a squeezy bottle of moisturiser. A running machine is running all on its own. A strange hairy object floating in a footspa turns out, on cautious inspection, to be a man's wig.

'Si, I think the people here left in a hurry. It's like they couldn't get out of here fast enough.'

'Given what's just happened on the stairs,' says Si, 'that hardly seems surprising.'

'But it does mean things are much worse here than people outside realise,' I say. 'No wonder I couldn't get in before. Whoever owns the Shard must be pretty desperate if they think Venn Specter and his rubbish TV show can help.'

On the wall near a receptionist's desk, beside an overly tasteful Christmas tree, is a plan of the

71

Shard – a spike-like schematic of the entire building. It's taller than I am.

'Where do you think we are now?' I say, my finger hovering at the midpoint of the map of the building.

'Oh, I don't know, Daniel.' Si puffs ectoplasm at me. 'Caught somewhere between Impossible Odds and Unspeakable Peril, I expect. We're certainly a long way south of Happily Ever After.'

'It looks to me like the hotel begins at Level 34,' I say, ignoring him. 'I wish I'd counted how many floors we climbed from the lift, but my guess is we're at the top of the hotel now, around here – level 52.'

I stare in dismay at the rest of the building towering up to the top of the map. I'm still puffed out from climbing over twenty levels just to get here, but I've got at least that much again to get back to the viewing level. And that's only if I can find another way onto the stairs and avoid being crushed to death by more falling furniture. In the meantime, what's happening to Stacey?

'You know what, Si? It seems to me that if we can't get up to see this "pretty lady", we're just going to have to get her to come down to see us somehow. I

72

think it's about time to we came to face-to-face with her ladyship, don't you?'

'But, Daniel…' Si starts to splutter. 'Are you sure that's wise?'

'Well, I suppose you could always fly up there on your own, Si. You know, take a look around, see what we're up against.'

Si goes whiter than an advert for washing powder.

'I think it would be better if we didn't split up,' he squeaks, his ectoplasm going small with fright. 'In fact, I'm beginning to think we should make a tactical retreat, Daniel. Maybe it was a mistake getting involved in this, after all.'

'Mistake or not, we can't wuss out now, Si. Do you really want to leave Stacey up there, with Death knows what, and only Venn and his stupid jade ring to save her?'

'Of course not!' Si splutters, a little ashamed of himself. 'But the risk, Daniel! It's my job to keep you safe. If anything happens to you, it would all have been for nothing!'

I turn to him. Once again I am reminded that there are things he's keeping from me, things he wouldn't let Mrs Binns say. I feel something in my deep coat pockets and realise that I still have that old copy of the Radio Times rolled up in there.

'All *what* would have been for nothing, Si? What is the big secret?'

Si slams his skeletal jaw shut and looks cross with himself.

'And anyway,' he says eventually, 'how on earth can you get the poltergeist to come down here? I don't see how it's even possible, so…'

'Well, it's funny you should ask that,' I say, adjusting my specs. 'Remember that plan you asked about earlier?'

'You said there wasn't one.'

I shrug.

'There is now.'

9

HOW TO SUMMON A GHOST

'It's something Tim said,' I explain. 'And, though he didn't realise it at the time, something Venn said too.'

'Something that will bring the poltergeist down here?' Si looks doubtful.

'Or at least provoke a reaction,' I say. 'You know what ghosts are like, Si – they all want something. Even you have something keeping you here, some purpose, even if you want to keep it secret from me.'

'Yes, well,' Si says. 'You're right about that, at least.'

'Yeah. And with most ghosts it's something they've left unsaid or undone, something I can help them with. And they can get pretty angry if I can't help, or of they've been waiting too long. Well, this is probably the angriest ghost we've ever come across. But even if I can't help her, there must still be a reason for that anger. That's why I asked Tim if he'd said anything to provoke the pencil attack in the gift shop.'

'Ah, so you did!' Si screws up his face to try and recall my conversation with Tim. The ectoplasm puffs from his head with the effort. 'He said something about his supervisor, he called her a… a "right nasty old…"'

'Exactly!' I say quickly, to stop Si from finishing it. 'And that's when the window cracked, remember? Then, what did Venn shout above the wind, just before the glass shattered completely and we were driven out of the viewing level?'

Si screws up his face again, but I know he has a good memory, despite dying from a musket ball in the brain. His face lights up.

'Oh!' he cries.

'Exactly,' I say again. 'It's not the same word really, but it *sounds* the same. And Venn shouted it out at least twice.'

Si looks at me, and I look back at him. Well, there's nothing to do but try it, is there?

I notice that the gym's exercise bikes are firmly bolted to the floor. I climb onto one and grab the handles tightly, bracing myself for whatever happens next. Then I shout the word as loudly as I can.

'Witch!'

Nothing happens.

But wait! Isn't there a slight change in the atmosphere? And are the hairs on the back of my neck starting to stand up?

'Witch!' I shout again, though slightly more timidly. 'Nasty old, er… witch?'

The atmosphere fizzes.

There's a flash of light as a vivid arc of electricity leaps from a power point on a nearby wall and connects with the exercise bike I'm sitting on. I find myself flying backwards through the air, my whole body singing with pain. I crash to the ground somewhere or other and lie there trying to work out which way is up and what my name is.

Someone is shouting, 'Daniel? Daniel?' I look

up and see that it's Si. Either my eyesight has been ruined, or even the emergency lights are out now. I can only see the ghostly glow of Simon in the pitch dark.

And another glow from something else.

I manage to move my arms enough to sit up, and turn my groggy head towards the new light. I see a figure standing across the other side of the gym, crackling and popping with electrical energy that pours out from the light fittings and plugs, and gathers in the form of a person.

The 'pretty lady'.

Actually, she's barely a lady at all, she's a teenage girl with cropped hair and a simple white dress.

But she is pretty. Mind you, being lit up like a Christmas tree probably helps with that.

'Grgnn…!' I manage to say through teeth that feel welded shut from the electric shock. What I want to say is 'hold your fire, I'm here to help', but 'grgnn' will have to do for the moment.

Si is hopping from one foot to the other, chewing his spectral finger nails, so there'll be no chance of a translation from him.

'Brbrgh…' I add, getting up onto my shaking legs and somehow managing to stand. My tongue is starting to move again too. 'Brbyuyu… hwelp… hwelp you. I can… help you.'

The electrical girl flashes with a pulse of angry power and her eyes narrow.

'Help me?' she cries with a fizzing voice. 'I have waited over four hundred years for help. None came. Now I will help myself.'

She gestures towards me with one of her hands. I just have time to drop to the floor as a bolt of lightning connects the girl's finger tips with the wall behind me in an explosion of heat and light. I see Simon caught in the attack. I have no idea what the relationship between ghosts and electricity is, but it can't be anything good because Simon explodes in a puff of ectoplasm and is gone. Burning wood and chunks of shattered marble rain down all around me, and the air smells like a demon's armpit.

'Four hundred years?' I say, peering over the seat of a rowing machine. My hair feels funny. I reach up and find it's standing straight up from my head. 'That is a long time to wait. So, er, something happened to you in sixteen hundred and, er, *something*, then?'

Okay, as conversation openers go this is pretty rubbish, I know, but I've got to keep her talking. This might be my only chance to find out what this whole business is about. The girl is crossing the room towards me now, riding through the air on wings of lightning.

'1603,' the girl says in a voice like a shattering iceberg. 'They cried "witch" then too.' And she adds, in a sing-song tone, 'Witch, witch, burn the witch!'

The girl comes to a stop in the air above me. I look up and try my emergency grin, the one I reserve for moments of utter hopelessness. No, I don't think it'll make any difference either.

'But I wasn't a witch!' the girl says, showering me with sparks. 'Not a witch at all, but they burned me anyway, those men. Burned me to ashes. I wasn't a witch, but oh, the irony. Look what I have become now!'

And she begins to glow brighter and brighter, with a sound like a generator being turned up to max.

I get ready for some sort of final bone-melting zap. Well, there's not much else I can do, is there? But then, as suddenly they appeared, the arcs of power joining the girl to the national grid wink out. In a moment, the electricity shuts down entirely.

The girl stares at her hands in fury, an ordinary ghost of faintly glowing ectoplasm and unearthly regret once again.

'No!' she cries. 'Why does the power never last?'

I don't know if she's expecting me to answer that or not, but before I can say anything, I'm being pelted with cushions, books, Christmas decorations, a coffee percolator – anything moveable that the poltergeist can get her spectral hands on. In a moment I'm completely covered.

When I finally dig myself out from the burnt tinsel and ruin, she's gone.

And I'm all alone in the dark.

10

AND THE PRETTY LADY
HAS A NAME

I don't know how long I sit there, trying to get my thoughts straight, and my hair flat again. It's so dark I can hardly see my hands in front of my face. I reach into my pocket and pull out my ghost-shaped keyring torch.

Okay, you can laugh, but right now I'm just glad I have it with me.

In the small light from the torch, I see that the gym

is in chaos, though I knew that already. What I'm not ready for is the fine layer of frost that is covering everything. The place is freezing! The foot spa with the wig in it is frozen solid, and my breath puffs out in white clouds as I take it all in.

And I'm seriously baffled by all this. I know some ghosts can move small objects with their minds, because I've seen Si do it. I know that ghosts can interfere with electrical currents, as well as make the room temperature drop. But everything I've seen here so far goes way beyond those slight things. How can the ghost of a teenage girl, even one four hundred years old, have so much bump-in-the-night power?

1603. That was what she said, wasn't it? And burnt as a witch? I've really got to get on the internet.

But when I reach the sleek desktop computer at the gym's reception, it's completely dead. I wouldn't be surprised if every computer in the building was burnt out in the electrical attack.

I go out through the main doors of the gym, and find myself in a corridor. Turning the torch onto the ceiling, I see that it's made of panels. I need to get up to the next floor somehow, to try and get onto the stairs again, above the blockage. And if I can't use the lift, I'm just going to have to go up directly through the ceiling.

It's as I'm dragging the receptionist's swivel chair into the corridor that Simon reappears.

Well, his head does at any rate. It appears in front of me looking startled and annoyed, trailing ectoplasm from his neck where the rest of his body should be.

'Hi, Si,' I say with a grin. 'Pull yourself together.'

'Ha ha.' Si's head grumps at me. 'Thank you for your concern.'

'Oh, I knew you'd be all right,' I say. 'After all, you're dead already. What's the worse that could happen?'

'I could have been spread across half the city!' Si snaps, as a pair of eighteenth-century buckled shoes appear on the ground at about the place where Si's feet should be. 'So when you've quite finished having fun at my expense, perhaps you'd like to explain what we're going to do next. While I look for my legs.'

'We've got to help her, Si,' I say, climbing up onto the chair, and pushing up one of the ceiling tiles.

'Well, of course we've got to get little Stacey down again, but – '

'I don't just mean Stacey. The girl in the white dress – she's so angry. She needs my help too.'

'That's very commendable,' says Si, blinking in surprise, 'but she died more than four hundred years ago. How can you possibly help her now? Some ghosts are beyond our help, Daniel, you know that.'

'Yeah, I know, but this one has just destroyed a luxury gym in the biggest skyscraper in London. I'm not exactly sure we can just walk away.'

'At least the authorities had the good sense to evacuate the building.'

'And that's another thing,' I say, as I pull myself up into the hollow space inside the ceiling. 'What about Venn Specter and his crony, Ned? They may be a pair of chumps, but they're putting themselves right in the firing line. And they don't even believe in ghosts! No, Si, however you look at it, someone has to defuse this situation before it really gets out of hand. And once again, it looks like that someone is going to be me.'

'Ahem.' Si gives his best butler's cough.

'I meant "us", Si,' I call back down from the hole in the ceiling. 'Obviously, I meant "us".'

Simon sniffs.

'Now make yourself useful,' I say. 'Ghost up into the level above and give me the all-clear. I don't want to climb up into another electrical storm, do I?'

'Indeed not, Master Dyer,' says Si, and he drifts up through the ceiling. After a moment, his disembodied hand appears right in front of me, and gives the thumbs-up sign. I push at the floor panel above me, and shove it to one side. In a single bound, I leap up into the next level of the Shard, and crouch in the dark, listening out for trouble.

Silence.

Except for the sounds of a storm raging outside.

I turn the torch onto my surroundings.

'We're in an apartment,' I whisper, as I take in the sophisticated, open-plan space. I see a giant-screen television, and a leather sofa the size of a yacht. Beyond the floor to ceiling windows, flurries of white snowflakes are being picked out in flashes of lightning from the sky above. The 'pretty lady' may have burnt out the wiring in the Shard, but it looks like she's found another source of electrical power. I start throwing cushions off the sofa and rummaging in cupboards.

'What are you doing, Daniel?'

'We need to work out what to do next,' I say, moving into a bedroom. 'And for that, we need some answers.'

'Well, I hardly think you'll find them in there,' he

calls, in a disapproving voice, as I rummage through a drawer full of frilly underwear. 'What *are* you looking for?'

I dash back out and head for the kitchen, which is vast and gleaming, and... there! I find what I'm after. I pick it up and wave it at Si.

'Ah, one of those miniature windows of wonder!' He gives a gasp of joy and zooms over to me.

'Almost, Si,' I say. 'It's a tablet – a kind of mini computer – and if we're lucky... yes! It's still charged up.'

I prop the tablet up on the marble worktop in the kitchen, and open a browser. The bar that indicates an internet connection is fluctuating wildly, but I manage to get online.

I type a few words into the search field...

WITCH+BURNT+LONDON+1603

... and dab 'return'.

There's a pause while the machine deals with the dodgy signal. Then results appear, a right mixed bag, and I start scrolling through them. I quickly realise it'll take me hours to find anything relevant in this lot, if I can't refine the search a bit more.

'Si, have you any idea why this poltergeist – this "pretty lady" – can be so much more powerful than a normal ghost?' I ask. 'Could she be a real, you know…' I spell out the word "witch" with my lips. 'I mean, could this be actual magic she's using?'

Simon snorts.

'Hardly, Daniel. There is no such thing as magic in the sense you mean. Everything we've seen her do so far is merely a magnification of the things all ghosts can do anyway.'

'A magnification?'

'Yes. As you know, all ghosts have a stronger presence in the place where they died. 'Tis possible that this presence could be further magnified in some way. For example, much has been written in the ancient texts of the spirit-boosting properties of crystals. Indeed, the Great Poojam of Kathmandu once wrote that…'

I stare at Si. A lightbulb has just gone on in my head.

'Si, what did you just say?'

'About the Great Poojam?'

'No! The bit about the "spirit-boosting crystals".'

'Well, 'tis said that placing a ring of crystals round the place a ghost died can strengthen its presence.'

'Yes! And what was it you said when you first saw the Shard up close, Si? That it was like a…'

Si's wig almost leaps off his head as he remembers.

'A monstrous great crystal!'

'Exactly. So what if *this* is where the "pretty lady" died?' I point down at the floor. 'What if this whole glass building is her place?'

'But Daniel, the Shard was only built a few years ago. How can she have died in it four hundred years in the past?'

'Not *in* it, Si. *Under* it.'

Si's mouth falls open. It's not a pretty sight.

'Think about it,' I go on. 'This poor girl is burnt to a crisp four hundred years ago, and gets left behind as a ghost. Years pass and nothing much happens. We don't even know she's there. No electrical blasting or weird storms – nothing. Just an ordinary ghost. Then they go and build this whacking great crystalline building over the place where she died, and...'

'... and suddenly we're dealing with the most powerful ghostly presence we've ever known.' Si punches the palm of his spectral hand. ''Zooks, Daniel! You're right! So all we have to do is get her away from the building and she'll be a normal ghost once again. If only the Great Poojam could have seen this...'

I wave my hand to silence him, and dab more words into the search field:

WITCH+BURNT+LONDON+SHARD+1603

A few results appear, and the uppermost one seems immediately interesting. It's the blog of a local historian with pebble glasses and a brightly-patterned pullover. I'm guessing this is normally a pretty lonely corner of the internet, but right now there's nowhere else in cyberspace I'd rather be. I'm staring at a blog post about a young witch who was burnt in 1603, right slap bang in the middle of what would later be the building site of the Shard. I'm even staring at a scan of the original court proceedings, which state, in heavy old-fashioned writing, that the defendant was found guilty of 'witchcrafte and strange comportmente'. Whatever that is. And there's a name.

'Mary Flaxen,' I say aloud. 'Her name is Mary.'

'Yes, but Daniel,' says Si, looking suddenly worried. 'About the giant crystal theory – there's something else you need to know…'

But before he can finish, the words die on his blue lips. He stares right past my left ear. Slowly, he raises his finger to point behind me.

I feel a chill run down my back. And I mean this

literally – it's like someone has just dropped an ice cube into my T-shirt. The screen of the iPad in my hands blooms with frost as the air temperature plummets.

I turn round.

II

MARY FLAXEN

'You called me,' she says. 'You know my name?'

The 'pretty lady' is standing in the doorway to the apartment. I'm pleased to say that right now she isn't crackling with energy and destroying the world around her just by looking at it. In fact, she looks just like an ordinary ghost, although there is a definite electrical charge in the atmosphere. I need to act fast if I'm going to keep things on a less-than-lethal level.

'Er…' I say, stepping back and raising my hands a little. 'Hi, Mary.'

'You can see me?' she says, looking confused. 'Even without the lightning power? No one has seen me like this for over four centuries. Who are you?'

'I'm Dan. This is my associate, Simon.' Si gives his frilliest bow. 'And like I tried to say earlier, we're here to help.'

'And as I told you, I don't need help from anyone.' Her face darkens, and a couple of static sparks dance amongst the designer copper pots and pans hanging in the kitchen. 'How did you find my name?'

I hold up the tablet computer, wondering if I need to explain what it is to someone from the age of the quill pen and Shakespeare. But before I can speak, the tablet is tugged out of my hand by some unseen power, and floats over to Mary. It spins in front of her till she can see the screen. I remember that the transcript of her trial for witchcraft is still displayed there.

Oops.

With an angry gesture, Mary pulls a bright arc of power from the tablet's battery. Then she lets it fall to the ground, where it clatters dead on the marble floor.

'Everything in this time,' she says, 'has the spark of lightning in it.'

''Tis called "electricity", miss,' Si explains, stepping forward and putting on his best schoolteacher manner. 'A most useful phenomenon, which...'

Si's voice is drowned out by a boom of thunder that roars around the building outside. Mary is glaring daggers at him.

'Do not call me that!'

'Call you what?' Si looks confused.

'Witch!'

'But I... oh!' Si snaps his mouth shut.

'The little girl,' I say quickly, steering the conversation away from witches, however they're spelled. 'Stacey. Why have you taken her?'

'She is young,' Mary declares, holding her head high. 'Her body is healthy. It is what I require.'

I exchange glances with Si.

'Require? What do you require her body for?'

'Fool!' Mary flashes with power, sending the copper pans dancing on their hooks. 'It is not complicated. My own body was destroyed by fire. Therefore I require a new one, I deserve a new one. The girl Stacey is my chance to live again.'

'But...' I can't believe what I'm hearing. 'You can't do that!'

'You think you can stop me?'

'No, I mean, you can't do that! It's not possible.' I turn to my side-kick. 'Er… is it, Si?'

'Oh, it is theoretically possible,' Si says, still in schoolteacher mode. 'Given sufficient power, and…'

'Si!'

I'd kick him in the shins at this point, if he still had any solid enough to kick. He gets the hint, but just a little too late.

'Oh, er… *no*, 'tis not possible, not possible at all,' he says quickly, through a desperate grin. 'It could never be done, not ever, so… er… don't even try. At all. Um…'

Mary gives a shriek of manic joy, and sends a playful arc of electricity skipping across the sofa, destroying it and filling the room with acrid smoke.

'I knew it could be done!' she cries. 'And I have the power.' She makes a motion as if to take off up through the ceiling.

'No, wait!' I shout. 'You can't do this to her! Stacey has done nothing wrong. She's innocent.'

Mary crackles.

'Innocent! I too was innocent. And yet look what they did to me. Burnt for a witch!'

'I'm really sorry that happened, Mary.' I say. 'It's horrible what they did to you. I understand, but...'

'You understand!' There's another boom of thunder, even louder than before, as a riot of lightning flickers beyond the windows. It's so cold now that every surface in the apartment is growing ice crystals. 'How can you possibly understand?'

'Then tell me!' I shout back, knowing that only by talking can I keep Mary here. If she leaves now, I'll never catch her in time to stop her doing Death-knows-what to Stacey. 'Talk to me. I've helped ghosts before. There must another way.'

Mary stops crackling and sparking. She gives me a look of sudden sadness and despair.

'You really want to understand what I have been through? You really want to know?'

I nod. Well, actually, I *don't* really want to know, because it all sounds so tragic and horrible, but nodding seems to be the only way to keep Mary away from Stacey, so I nod again.

Mary raises one eyebrow.

'Would you like to *see?*'

I keep nodding, and manage to glance at Si. All he can do is shrug back. What does she mean, see?

Mary raises her hand. Slim tendrils of lightning leap from her fingers, and crawl over my scalp. My teeth clamp together. But this is not simply electricity – there's ectoplasm mixed in there too. It's something I've never experienced before. My eyesight goes blurry.

'Then, boy,' comes the voice of Mary, 'I will show you.'

The tendrils of power reach into my mind.

Everything goes dark

12

THE GHOST OF
CHRISTMAS PAST

The next thing I see is a street scene. But I don't mean cars and taxis and lamp posts; the ground beneath me is cobbled, and the houses are thatched. A horse passes just a few centimetres from my nose, pulling a cart full of barrels.

I blink, and stare around, trying to work out what's happening. Half-timbered buildings with dark little windows loom over me. This doesn't look like anywhere I've ever been before, and yet I know this is London because I suddenly recognise the towers of Westminster Abbey rising into the sky above the roof tops. But that's just about all I recognise.

Mary is standing next to me, but she's no longer a tower of electrical fury. In fact, she looks like a living girl now: all smudge-faced defiance and cropped blonde hair. Something tells me I'm seeing her the way she was the day she died.

'What is this?' I say. 'Where are we?'

'You said you wanted to see,' Mary replies. 'So, boy, let me take you on a guided tour of my memories. Welcome to Christmas Day, 1595.'

I admit, I'm pretty much goggling now. I'm seeing the past?! Even if it is just some illusion, right now it looks and feels exactly as if I'm standing right in it, horse droppings and all. I can even smell the clogged drainage ditch in the middle of the cobbled street (though I wish I couldn't).

As I watch, a man dressed in sumptuous clothing, with an immense white collar and blue velvet hat, emerges from the door of a tall town house opposite us. He steps over a puddle of something unspeakable as if he doesn't even see it, and strides out into the street. Behind him comes a little blond boy, wearing a miniature version of the man's costume, complete with the hat.

'Who do you think these people are?' says Mary, pointing.

I look again at the man and the small boy hurrying behind him, and shrug.

'Something tells me that isn't Bob Cratchit and Tiny Tim.'

'I know of no Bob Cratchit,' Mary says. 'That is my father, hurrying to church. The boy dressed like a prince is my brother.'

Then behind the boy, a line of girls with covered heads and simple white dresses and cloaks emerge from the house and hurry after man. Each one is shorter than the last. The very last one, who is tiny, trips over her cloak, and has to be helped up by one of her sisters.

'I am barely six years old,' says Mary, pointing to the little one. 'No more than a scrap.'

'Why are you showing me this?' I say, as we watch the little version of Mary trot after her family and vanish into the crowd.

'My father is a merchant in the city of London. Not the richest, perhaps, but a man of substance nevertheless. He is desperately proud of my brother.

After all, it took him five attempts to have a son.'

'Oh. You mean…?'

'Yes, I was the last attempt.' Mary glowers at me. 'Even at that age, I already knew I wasn't wanted. Nothing but a failed boy.'

'Where's your mother?' I ask, hoping to move things on to happier territory.

'Dead.' Mary looks down. 'She died giving birth to my brother.'

Ah, crapsticks.

'Okay, Mary – this is really terrible,' I say, and I mean it. 'But it still doesn't give you the right to have Stacey.'

'I haven't finished yet.' Mary waves her hand, causing the image of the world to reel around us. 'Now we will jump forward to a later memory.'

The picture whirls crazily before it re-settles into the view of another place entirely: the interior of a large room, with a fire roaring in the grate of an immense carved fireplace. Mary's father is sitting at a table, lit by candles. He is talking to Mary's brother.

'He looks older,' I say, whispering though I know they can't possibly hear us. 'Your brother. What's the date now?'

'We are now in the year 1600. I have only three years left to live.'

'But where are you? Where are your sisters?'

Mary gives an angry snort.

'The two eldest are married off, as cheaply as possible. The next oldest is in her room, awaiting the same fate.'

'And you?'

'Little me?' Mary says, bitterly. 'I've already been sold.'

'*Sold?*'

'Well, as good as. They called it an apprenticeship, but I was a slave in all but name. My father just wanted me gone. He had his son and heir. I should be many miles from this place, wearing my fingers to the bone in a tailor's workshop, sewing undergarments for rich ladies.'

There's suddenly a note of mischief in her voice.

I turn to her. 'Should be? Why do you say "should be"?'

Mary flashes her eyes again.

'Watch and see.'

I turn back to the scene before us.

Mary's father seems to be explaining some paperwork to her brother. The boy looks bored.

Then there's a knock at the door. The father calls 'Come!', and the door opens to allow in a second boy. He's slight of build and quick, this newcomer. He stops neatly before the great desk, his hands behind his back.

I wonder why I'm being shown this other boy. Then a realisation hits me. I dash forward, so I can see the boy's face again. It takes me a moment to be sure, but then I cry out to Mary, 'But that's you! I thought it was a boy, but…'

'Of course you did,' Mary declares. 'Everyone thinks he's a boy, that's the point. But it is me, with my hair cut short and my legs in breeches. My father is so uncaring and my brother so witless that they have no idea they have employed me as their messenger boy. I ran away from that tailor and his terrible workshop, and through my own cleverness and trickery I became a trusted member of my father's own household. And he has no idea.'

I look again at the messenger boy, who is really Mary in disguise. Mary's father folds a letter and passes it to him. I see the boy – Mary – take it, bow, and then dash out of the room.

'But why did you do all this?'

'Only a boy could ask such a stupid question!'

Mary snaps. 'As an unwanted girl, I was nothing. But as a boy, even a boy servant...'

Mary waves her hand, and the view changes once more, slipping by so that we can follow her disguised self as she runs through the streets, still clutching the letter. We watch her leap up steps, weave between bustling carriages, even jump between low boats on the Thames. At one point she steals a ripe pear from a silver bowl on the lap of a fat man who is being carried in a chair. The man shouts, but Mary is already gone, eating the pear in delight as she runs.

'Freedom!' Mary cries. 'This is why I did it. No petticoats or needlework. No limits. Of all my father's children, I was surely the brightest! But he could see no further than the cap on my dim brother's head. At least I had the chance to take their money and make fools of them both.'

'Mary, what happened?' I ask, though part of me doesn't want to know. I mean, let's face it, we all know this is a story with a really bad ending. For Mary, that is.

'Keep watching,' Mary says in a small voice. She waves her hand, making the picture swirl again. 'We will jump forward to the day it all went wrong.'

The world resolves once more, and now we are

in a corridor with a black and white tiled floor. We see Mary's brother in his silk clothes burst through a door, and run down the corridor yelling. Then Mary runs out after him, calling him back. She looks like she's only just pulled on her shirt.

'In the end it was my own stupid body that gave me away. I was fourteen when they found me out. Even my brother wasn't thick-headed enough to miss the obvious signs that I was becoming a woman.'

'But did he recognise you?'

'I honestly don't think he did,' Mary says. 'Maybe if he had he wouldn't have shouted about it so much. But as it was, by the time he'd calmed down, he'd given away my secret to every servant and guest in the house. I was exposed as an imposter – a girl who had so successfully disguised herself as a boy that some said only magic could explain it.'

'*That's* why you were called a witch?' I can hardly believe my ears. 'But that's ridiculous.'

'Of course it is! But no one wanted to admit they had been taken in by a simple disguise. My father, least of all. So I was branded a subtle and dangerous witch, even before I was led from the house by the constable.'

The image jumps forward again, to show Mary

being thrust into the belly of a greasy black carriage with barred windows.

'But how can people be so stupid?' I say.

'It was a plague year.' Mary gives a four-hundred-year-old sigh. 'People were frightened. And people wanted to believe it. A witch is a nice thing to blame all your ills on, after all. The charges against me stacked up quickly. I was guilty of everything from cursing our neighbour with pimples to causing the river to flood through dark enchantments.'

The view changes again, as Mary speaks, moving fast now from one scene to another. First we're in a cell, with Mary alone on a bench. Then we're in a courtroom of some kind, with austere men in tall black hats and starched white collars, spitting as they shout accusations at her. Then Mary is taken away, then her hands are bound. Then we see a pile of wood and branches piled in a tall cone around a wooden post...

'Okay, okay!' I shout. My heart is pounding, and I'm sick with the dizzying changes in the images from Mary's memory. And I really don't want to witness how this ends. 'I've seen enough.'

'What's wrong, boy?' Mary purrs in my ear. 'I thought you said you wanted to understand.'

'Yeah, but you've made your point,' I say. 'I don't want to… I just don't want to see…'

'What?' Mary stares straight into my face. 'You don't want to see me burn? Burn *alive?*' And she makes an angry gesture with her hand.

The wooden post and the pile of bonfire are in a small square surrounded by houses. People are crowding around, jeering. Mary is already tied to the post. A man in a black hood is holding a burning torch. The air smells of oil and sweaty people and death.

'Mary!' I shout. 'No!'

The hooded man puts the torch to the wood at Mary's feet.

I close my eyes, as tight as I can.

But I can still see. The branches crackle as the fire takes hold. Soon the flames climb higher, wreathing around the girl with the cropped blonde hair and the simple white dress. The blood is roaring in my ears. There's a scream, but by now I don't know if it's Mary or me.

I feel like I'm falling.

I feel like I'm *burning.*

'Stop!'

13

VENN AGAIN

'Stop!'

I open my eyes, and find I'm lying on the floor of the modern apartment in the Shard once more, shouting. Well, I suppose this is where I always was. I struggle to my feet, blinking.

'What have you done to him?' Si is demanding. 'Daniel, what happened to you?' Mary ignores him, and I'm not sure how to explain what I've just seen.

'So.' The ghost of Mary stands in the centre of the

room, crackling with a dangerous charge of electrical power once more. 'Now do you understand? I am owed a new life, boy – a second chance. And for that I need Stacey's body. I deserve it. And with me she will be powerful beyond anything she can imagine.'

'But she's only a tiny kid,' I say, straightening my specs. 'I doubt she imagines much beyond where the next doughnut's coming from.'

'Then what is there for her to lose?'

'Only everything you yourself lost,' I snap back. Well, I'm beginning to get annoyed with all this. 'Yes, it was terrible what happened to you, Mary, and yeah, I guess you deserve a second chance. But Stacey deserves that too. She hasn't even had her *first* chance yet!'

Mary sets her jaw and stares at me. She's crackling as scarily as ever, but something in her eyes suggests she knows I'm right. I don't miss my opportunity.

'She's like you were in that first scene you showed me,' I say. 'Small, and just trying to keep up with the grown-ups. You know what it feels like to be her, Mary. You remember. And that's why I don't think you can ever do anything to hurt Stacey.'

Mary looks down at her hands as they crackle with electrical power.

'But it's all so… *unfair!*'

'I know it is.' I step forward. 'But you're a good person, Mary. Don't be unfair to Stacey.'

I've got through to her, I can tell. She glances up and I manage to catch her eye.

'Bring Stacey to me, Mary,' I say, as gently as I can. 'Please. Let me take her down to safety. Then, I promise, I will do all I can to help you.'

Mary lowers her hands, defeated. She lets out a fizzing, spectral sigh. But then, just as she's about to speak again, the worst thing that could possibly happen at this precise moment… happens.

'Oh my God, are you getting this, Ned, *are you getting this?*' Venn Specter shouts out as he edges into the room. He's staring in complete astonishment at the column of crackling electrical power in the shape of a girl. And you don't need to be able to see ghosts to see *that*, believe me. Ned walks in behind him, his mouth hanging open. The lens of his camera is on me and Mary, the little red recording light blazing.

'Ladies and gentlemen!' Venn looks like he can't believe what his eyes are showing him, but as he warned me earlier, he's not going to let an opportunity like this get away. 'You see before you proof – *proof,* I tell you! – that ghosts exist! They actually exist! I, Venn Specter, have brought you face to face with the nameless evil that is haunting the Shard. The devilish presence that is terrorising this place, which…'

Mary blazes with light, all sense of being swayed by my words forgotten.

'Mary, wait!' I shout, but it's no good. She rises off the ground, her arms outstretched, her back to me now as she turns to face Venn.

'Dear viewers, you are seeing history being made.' Venn really doesn't know when to shut up, does he? He even scurries round in front of the camera so that he can be in the same shot as Mary. 'A real live evil spirit! And it is I, Venn Specter, who investigated it.'

As selfies go, this one's pretty suicidal.

The windows of the apartment explode inwards. A bolt of lightning from the sky connects with Mary, who pours power out from her fingers in countless arcs of electricity. The whole flat erupts in light and flame and destruction, and I hit the deck.

When I next look up, Venn and Ned are in the air, floating upside down. Venn is screaming. Ned's eyes are bulging out from his head, but the camera's still at his shoulder, filming the lot.

'Mary, stop!' I shout, but I doubt she can hear me now with the crackle of power, and the wind and snow that's roaring in through the windows.

'I am not evil!' Mary's voice booms with the power of thunder. 'And I. Am not. A WITCH!'

With a final pulse of electrical power, she rushes out through the ruined window and into the night sky beyond the building. With a cry of panic, Venn is pulled out after her, still upside down, his legs pinned together by a thick band of ice. Ned flies out behind him, still filming. Then all three rush up and out of sight, as Mary takes two more captives up to the summit of the Shard.

'I nearly had her, Si,' I say, still sitting on the floor. I punch the ruined sofa in anger. 'Then that numpty showed up and turned it all into Halloween again.'

'You mustn't blame yourself,' Si says. 'I warned you that Mary might be too far gone. Four hundred years of frustration and then this sudden great power. I don't think she can resist it.'

'I'm not accepting that, Si.' I get to my feet. 'And I'm not giving up and running away.'

'But Daniel, there's something you need to know.'

'What?' I snap, still annoyed. I remember now that he was trying to tell me something before Mary appeared.

'Well, if we're right that Mary's great power is derived from the building, that the Shard itself is magnifying her in some way, then there's no reason I can see why her power will ever stop growing.'

'What do you mean?'

'I mean that she will simply grow stronger and stronger until either she gets the new body she wants and leaves this place, or until she destroys the building entirely. And probably a sizable portion of central London at the same time.'

I goggle at him.

'Are you serious?'

'Daniel, Mary is a four-hundred-year-old bundle of fury and resentment, fuelled by a spirit battery the size of a volcano. We need to be as far away from here as possible when that volcano erupts.'

'No, Si. I'm not leaving, and I'm not just letting her have Stacey either.'

'But what can you do?' Si is flapping again.

'I'm going to do what I always do,' I say, straightening my lapels and setting my purple specs. 'Come up with an awesome plan. But first, we need to get up to the top of this building.'

Simon looks appalled.

'But how?' he cries. 'You can't use the lift, the stairs are a death trap – how will you ever get to the top floor?'

I look around the flat. The wind is still roaring in through the shattered windows, and snow is already banking up around the singed and ruined furniture. There's a flash and a clap of thunder as I turn to Si.

'With a little help from a friend.'

14

A RUBBISH PLAN

'Daniel, you aren't serious?' Si's skeletal jaw nearly falls off his face.

'Why not?' I say. 'Mrs Binns got me into the Shard in the first place. I reckon she can help me get to the top of it now.'

'You got *yourself* in here.' Si looks really angry now. 'All that old woman did was set you on the right track.'

'Exactly,' I say. 'Mrs Binns has a way of making

you look at things again, of turning problems into opportunities. And frankly, Si, the only vibe I'm getting off you right now is frilly negativity and gloom.'

'Daniel!' Si bristles. 'That is most unfair.' But I'm already heading off into the less trashed parts of the flat, searching around.

'It is my job to see you are safe and protected…' Si goes on, catching up with me in the bathroom. But I hold up my hand for silence.

There, in the corner of the bathroom, beneath a platinum toilet roll holder, is the object I seek.

A small, steel pedal bin.

'And what, pray, do you expect to find in that?' Simon couldn't sound more scathing if he tried. I glare back at him.

'A little can-do attitude,' I say. 'Even if it is trash-can-do.'

Si snorts and folds his arms.

I put my hand on the lid of the bin.

'Show me what to do, Mrs Binns,' I whisper.

Then I open the lid, and shine the ghost-shaped torch inside.

There's a white plastic bin bag with a used disposable razor in it. There's also an empty and curling toothpaste tube, a used sticking plaster, several screwed-up bits of tissue I *really* don't want to touch, and a lot of toenail clippings. I close the lid, then open it again, but nothing changes.

'Well?' I can almost hear the triumphant puffs of ectoplasm from Simon's head as he stares down behind me. 'What have you found? A grappling hook? A magic carpet? A pair of angel wings to whisk you into the sky?'

'Shut up, Si, I'm trying to think.'

'Think?' Simon blazes spookily at me. 'You're looking for a plan in a dustbin! That's not thinking at all, that's just desperate.'

'Shut up, Si!'

'No! Daniel, we have to leave. This case is too big for us, Mary is too far gone. There's nothing we can do now but get you away from here, away to safety…'

I chuck the bin at Si's head. Well, I'm fed up with all his whining, aren't I? Of course, the bin just flies through him harmlessly, and bangs off the wall, but he still deserves it. The bag of crud falls out, and spills onto the floor.

'That's all the thanks I get?' Simon gasps. 'After all I've done to help you? A bin bag in the face?'

'Yeah, well, maybe I'm fed up with your help,'

117

I shout back. Outside, the thunder and lightning make the building boom. At least it's a good backdrop for an argument. 'And being told to run away by a useless old dead guy with a pony tail is no help at all.'

'Oh, fine!' Si draws himself up to his full height. 'Well, if sir no longer requires my help, sir can jolly well manage without it!'

'Fine, yourself,' I snap back. 'Buzz off, then.'

Si gives me one last outraged sniff, and then vanishes in a puff of his most superior ectoplasm.

I'm alone in the bathroom, the storm still raging outside. The ruined pedal bin rolls around at my feet.

Ah, crapsticks.

'Si?' I say. But there's no reply.

I kick the bin as hard as I can, then slump in despair on the tiles.

Then I hear a baggy rustling sound.

I look up.

The bag from the pedal bin, now that it's empty, is hovering in the air above me, as if caught on a breeze. I shine the torch up at it. Maybe it's the dark or my imagination, I don't know, but for a moment – just a fleeting moment – I see a face in the folds of that bin bag. The gap-toothed and grinning face of someone I know.

'Mrs Binns?'

The bag rolls in the air as wind from the storm outside seizes it. Then it zips out through the bathroom door. In a moment, I'm on my feet and running after it.

'Mrs Binns!'

Back in the open-plan wreck of the apartment, I just have time to see the white bag fly out through the shattered window in a flurry of snow.

It's gone.

And now I really am all alone.

There's yet more flashing and booming of thunder, and I imagine that Mary is, even now, trying to force her mind into little Stacey's body so that she can live again. And there's not a single thing I can do about it.

Perhaps I really have failed this time.

Then something catches my eye, something fluttering just outside the window. I edge forwards, trying to make it out. The carpet is covered in a thick layer of snow now, which crunches underfoot. The wind stings my eyes. I reach the ragged edge of the floor, and gasp at the sight of London spread below me, without any glass or safety rail. One unlucky gust of wind and I could be out and falling to my death in a moment. But I just need to see what's flapping. I lean out, a little more…

It's the bag. The little white plastic bag from the pedal bin. And it's caught on something.

'Ropes?' I say aloud, staring in disbelief.

Then I remember what Tim said in the lift, about the Shard being cleaned by climbers who abseil down the side of the building. Sure enough, the bag is caught on a leather pouch attached to the rope – a pouch which still contains a ragged cloth and a 'Mr Squirty' bottle of cleaning fluid.

Taking firm hold of the window frame, I lean out even more and look up. The ropes rise away into the night. But in a flash of lightning, I see the silhouette of a metal frame right at the summit, the ropes reaching all the way up to it.

It's a way to the top of the Shard.

At that moment, the bin bag dislodges itself and flies off into the dark.

Now, I know what you're thinking. You're thinking that I'm mad to even contemplate climbing up these ropes. And yup, I admit there are a number of negative factors against the idea. Let's list them:

1. I'm hundreds of metres up the tallest skyscraper in Europe, with hundreds of metres still to go.
2. I'm a fourteen-year-old boy with a leather trench coat and a pair of purple specs, not Bear Grylls or James Bond or something.
3. There's the mother of all electrical storms raging and that rope looks wet, and… well, you get the picture.
4. There is no safety net.

I think I know what Si would say if he was here now.

But he's not here, is he? And beside, there's something else to add to that list, something that puts a more positive spin on the rest:

5. I'm the kid who sees dead people.

And over the years, those dead people have been good at paying me back for sorting out their problems.

I help them over to the Hereafter, and they give me something in return: a little piece of their memories and experience. After all, a bit of themselves is the only thing a ghost has left to pay me with. And that's how I know how to hack computers (useful), and speak French (interesting), and solve a Rubik's Cube (er…). And, because I once helped the ghost of a mountaineer, that's also how I'm able to look at these ropes and not freak out of my skull at the thought of climbing up them.

I do up my coat. I dig some leather gloves out of my pocket and slip them on. I grab the ropes.

Of course, knowing how to twist those ropes around my body and lock them over my arm like a pro is one thing. Not losing my cool over the scary view down is quite another. I close my eyes and think James Bond-type thoughts, but I'm still trying to get in the zone when the wind suddenly goes crazy and sucks me right out of the window.

'Aaagh crapsticks!' I cry out, as I bounce along the glass exterior of the Shard. 'I'm not in the zone, I'm not in the zone!'

The wind roars its reply in a blizzard of snow. By the time I stop bouncing, my nose is pressed up against the freezing glass, and my arms feel ready to pop out of their sockets. But the ropes are holding.

Then I look down…

'Gnn!'

I close my eyes again, and take a few desperate breaths. Forget James Bond, I need to focus on the borrowed memories of that dead mountaineer. This is the first time I've had to use them, so they're a bit hazy. Why couldn't I have helped the ghost of a lift mechanic instead? Anyway…

I open my eyes again. The icy wind blasts at my face, forcing snow up my nose and into my ears. My woolly scarf is flying out horizontally into the night. But somehow I manage to get my rubber soles firmly planted on the glass, and my body into position. I pull the rope in a very professional way, and pay out the slack as – against all the odds – I begin to climb.

15

TRASH CAN-DO

I don't know how long the ascent takes. It's all I can do to keep going in the blinding wind and snow. Below me, the Shard slopes away to the distant pavement. There's a glow down there that must be the crowd and the film crew and the giant screen in the square outside the entrance to the building. For a moment I wish I was down there too, eating a ketchuppy hotdog and listening to Christmas carols, and not dangling above certain and very messy death. Why is it always me who ends up dangling? I quite fancy a hotdog, for a change.

There's a rude squeak as my rubber soles slip on the glass, and I crash into it.

I'm exhausted.

The borrowed mountaineering skills have told me what to do, but my skinny fourteen-year-old body can no longer cope with the demands being made of it. I make a final effort, and manage to get up a couple more metres, but I slip again, and end up kissing the glass once more.

Except, no – it isn't glass. The surface of the building is wavy now, and icy cold. In fact, it *is* ice.

I open my eyes and try to get my bearings. As I blink in the snow, I guess that I must now be as high as the viewing level of the Shard.

But all the glass here was destroyed, I say to myself, thinking back to the moment we lost Stacey. *How…?*

Then I get it. Incredibly, sheets of wind-sculpted ice have formed over the shattered windows. In fact, I now see that the rest of the building above me is covered in one solid pyramidal cap of ice, enclosing the whole peak of the Shard. There is no way in that I can see.

So, I'll have to make my own.

I get my feet flat on the ice again, and stand out from the building, braced with the rope. I bend my legs and push away, swinging out into the stormy night. Gravity doesn't let me go for long though, and I'm soon crashing back into the ice. I have to do this three times before I hear a DINK sound, and see cracks appear. I give a final thrust with my legs, my arms screaming at me to stop. When I hit the ice this time, I break through, and tumble down onto the wooden floor of the viewing level.

I struggle to my feet. I'm inside the Shard again, but with the outer surface now made of ice, the interior is bitterly cold. Frosty blooms cover every surface with crystal forms that twinkle in the flashes of lightning. Santa would kill to have this as his grotto. If he could get here without being fried alive by the resident ghost, that is.

'Mary!' I shout.

No answer but the crash of thunder.

I head for the centre of the level, where the concrete core of the building continues up. There are frosted stairs here, and I limp up them as fast as I can, pulling my scarf close. When I reach the top of the stairs I stop in amazement at what I find there.

The very summit of the Shard is a square concrete platform, no bigger than my living room at home. On each side, a triangle of steel and glass rises up to form four flat spires. The spires don't touch though, allowing an opening to the snowy, stormy sky above.

Mary is floating up there, gathering power from the storm, filling the space with a dazzling electrical light.

In the middle of the platform, ice has been drawn up to form the bars of a glittering cage. In the cage sits Stacey, looking unfazed at the extraordinary things that are happening around her. She is wrapped in the folds of an enormous fur coat that must have come from one of the luxury flats beneath us. In front of her is an open box of Turkish delight. She pops a piece in her mouth, and points at me.

'The weirdy boy!' she squeals, with a puff of icing sugar.

Something moves at her words, and I see Ned. He's on the inside of one of the four triangular spires, welded in place by slicks of ice. His eyes are wild, but he manages to aim the camera at me, the red light still twinkling.

'Hi, Ned,' I say. 'The show must go on, I see.'

Opposite him, on another Spire, Venn Specter is

struggling against his own icy bonds. He makes faint 'hmm hmm!' noises, but a band of ice is completely covering his mouth.

'Well, Mary, I can forgive you that, at least,' I say, as I adjust my lapels and set the specs for action.

And it's now that Mary sees me.

'You?' she says, with a crackle of power. 'Why are you still here?'

'We, er, we were having a bit of chat, remember?' I say. 'Shame it got so rudely interrupted.' I give Venn one of my coldest stares. 'Thought we could pick up where we left off.'

Mary drifts down until she is floating just above the ice cage that contains Stacey. 'Pretty lady!' says Stacey, forgetting to eat a piece of Turkish delight in her admiration.

'There is nothing more to discuss,' Mary says in a blaze of light. 'I need only the time to fully understand how to take over the child's body. Since your frilly friend…'

'Si,' I point out. 'His name is Simon.'

'Since your friend *Simon* confirmed it can be done, I have made progress. Watch…'

Mary points down to Stacey. Small tendrils of light – like the ones she used on me to show her memories – extend from her hand until they dance around Stacey's head. Stacey lowers her hand from her face, still clutching a lump of Turkish delight, and turns to me. She opens her mouth to speak, but the words that comes out are all Mary's.

'I can already control the child. Her mind is not strong. I have only to make it permanent…'

'Stop!' I shout, and jump forward to the ice cage, grabbing the bars. 'Mary, get out of there! I thought we agreed you shouldn't do this.'

The tendrils of light retract.

'My name's not Mary!' Stacey shouts up at me, in control of herself again. She recoils into the furry coat. 'Why are you shouting at me, weirdy boy? Weirdy boy not nice!'

Mary laughs, but it's a hollow sound.

'Don't scare her, boy. Her fate is already sealed. Just turn around and leave.'

'But Mary, after all the things you showed me, all the stuff we said about fairness and unfairness – how is this fair to Stacey?'

Mary shakes her head.

'Life is unfair. I've had four hundred years to think about that. Now go, boy, before I tire of you.'

I watch Mary rise up to the apex of her ice

pyramid one again. I see Venn and Ned encased in ice, helpless. I look down at little Stacey. She sticks her tongue out at me.

I'd like to say that the faint glimmerings of a plan form in my mind, or, better still, that a brilliant idea comes to me in flash. But that doesn't happen. Instead I just feel cold and numb and defeated. Oh, and fed up. Yeah, really fed up.

Who does this ghost girl think she is?

'Witch!' I shout up at her.

Mary looks down at me, stunned.

'That's all you are,' I call up. 'Looks like those men who burnt you were right after all. I don't know why I bothered – you're nothing but a nasty, spiteful, child-snatching witch. So, yeah, I'm going…'

I put my foot through the bars of the cage, shattering them.

'… and I'm taking Stacey back to her mum.'

I reach in to get her out.

And that's when the bolt of lightning hits me.

I'm lifted clear off the floor and sent flying back. I smack into the ice sheet between two of the spires with a crash. The ice shatters, and I fly straight out into the night, propelled by Mary's fury. In no time at all, I'm well out into the sky beyond the Shard, with nothing between me and the crowded square below. I just have time to wonder if they've saved me a hotdog when I begin to fall.

16

CONTRARY MARY

My life doesn't flash before my eyes. Maybe that's because I haven't had enough of it yet. Fourteen is no age to die, after all, but then I guess Mary knows all about that.

No, all I can see, as G-force drags my eyelids back and makes my cheeks flap, is the top of a DazzleTV van in the square below as I race towards it like an incoming missile.

They'll be needing a new van.

I wonder if even my purple specs will survive to identify what caused the crater. Probably not.

I manage to close my eyes just before I hit.

But then…

I find myself opening them again.

At first I can't see anything other than grey, and I wonder if that's all there is to see after you die. Then I realise that it's the grey of the TV van I'm looking at. The surface of it is literally *one centimetre* away from my nose. I look down at my body, and find I'm hovering in the air!

But I don't even have time to say 'huh?' before I'm racing skyward again, like a crazy replay of my fall, only in reverse. My purple specs get dragged off my face, but I manage to grab them as I rocket back up into the night sky…

… and find myself being lowered, with surprising gentleness, through the hole in the tip of the ice pyramid at the summit of the Shard.

In a moment, I'm standing back on the concrete platform again, my legs trembling. After a few goes, I get my purple shades back on.

'Daniel!' Simon swoops over to me, and round and round. 'Oh, thank the Hereafter! I didn't know if she could stop you in time.'

'S-s-she?' I manage to say.

Si stops swooping.

'Mary,' he says. 'She was the only one with the power to break your fall.'

I look up at Mary. She is hovering above my reunion with Si, giving me a strange stare I can't understand.

I hear a squeal and see that Stacey – the cage of ice reformed around her – is clapping.

'Weirdy boy fly again! Weirdy boy fly again!'

'But…' I say, trying to work this out. 'Mary's also the one who just blasted me off the building.'

Mary drops lower, until she's floating in front of me.

'Is it true?' she says. 'What your friend Simon says? That you know how a ghost can take over a living body?'

My purple specs almost fall off again.

'What!?'

'Daniel, I had to tell her something!' Simon is grinning desperately. 'I had but moments, and so… I told her.'

I can't believe my ears. So *this* is why she saved me?

'When you help ghosts over to the Hereafter,'

Mary continues, 'they pay you with their memories? Is this true?'

'Well, yeah,' I say. 'Not all of their memories, obviously. Just a few useful skills or experiences.'

'But what if they *did* give you all of their memories?' Mary is getting closer. I don't like the glint in her eye. 'What would happen to you?'

I switch on the grin. I've often wondered this. How much of other peoples' memories could I take on before I stop being myself, and become, well... *them?*

I have no idea. But I also have no intention of finding out. That's why I keep it simple: one ghost helped = one memory paid. Job jobbed. And cheap at the price too, considering what I do for them.

'Look, thanks for saving me and all that, but you've got the wrong end of the stick,' I say to Mary. 'I know how *I* get paid to help ghosts, yeah? But I don't know how to get *you* into Stacey's head.'

'But I don't want to get into Stacey's head,' says Mary, dangerously sweetly. 'Not any more. You were right all along. She's just a little child. Whereas you...' Mary's eyes light up with glee. 'You are near full-grown. And a boy!'

'Er, yeah.' I manage to keep the grin in place

somehow. 'Last time I looked. Unless something's dropped off with the cold…'

'I felt such freedom when I dressed as a boy,' Mary continues, in a dreamy voice. 'Now I can put on the ultimate disguise. Your body is the body I need. And you even know how to give it to me.'

'Woah, let me stop you there!' I'm backing away. 'Hey, Si – thanks mate!' I call over to where Simon is floating.

'Forgive me, Daniel!' he wails. 'It was the best I could do. But at least I managed to buy you a few more seconds of life. Now you can have one of your amazing plans.'

'I will live again,' Mary croons, advancing towards me. 'And this time, I will be a boy! A slightly sickly looking one, it's true, and with stupid hair…'

'Oi!'

'… but a boy all the same. I will be free!'

'Look, Mary…' I say, backed right up against the ice sheet at the edge of the platform now, with nowhere else to go. 'I can still fight you, you know. If you try to get into my head. I can still resist.'

Mary laughs. She's so close, and crackling so brightly, that I have to close my eyes even behind my shades.

'You can always try,' she says.

I let my shoulders sag. I mean, who am I kidding? Mary is gaining power by the minute, whereas I'm exhausted after everything I've been through. What chance do I have against her?

So much for coming up with an awesome plan. I see Simon's still looking at me expectantly, but there's nothing I can do, not now Mary's made up her mind. Except, maybe there's one thing...

'Okay, Mary, okay,' I say, putting my hands up in defeat. 'But if I let you do this, then you don't need Stacey anymore, do you? You can let her go.'

Mary shrugs, then snaps her fingers.

An arc of electricity dances over Stacey's ice cage, destroying it in a cloud of glittering ice particles.

'Oooh!' says Stacey holding her hands out to catch them.

There's a 'hmmm hmmm HMM!' sound, and I see that Venn and Ned are still prisoners of the ice too.

'And the others?' I say. 'You'll let them go as well?'

'It is already done.' says Mary.

A second arc shatters the ice that's holding Venn, and then Ned. Venn falls in a heap, but springs to his feet.

'Ohmygodohmygodohmygod!' he cries, half hysterical. 'Ohmygod! Ned, are you getting this? We are going to be rich! Please say you're getting this!'

Ned staggers over to him, the camera still on his shoulder.

'Yes sir, I'm getting it, all right,' he says. 'I think I'm finally getting it loud and clear.'

Ned takes the camera off his shoulder and brings it crashing down onto Venn's head. Venn hits the concrete, out cold. Then Ned drops the power pack and cables, scoops Stacey up in his big bodyguard arms, and dashes off down the stairs to safety.

Mary doesn't even turn round to look at any of this. Her eyes are boring into mine.

'Relax, boy,' she says, lifting one hand to reach for my face. 'Just think of this as your payment for helping me, that's all. I'll try not to make it hurt.'

The tendrils of power creep over my scalp once again.

I hold up my finger to say one last witty thing that will stop all this madness and put the world to rights. But I don't even get the first word out. With a flash of light, Mary starts to fry my brain.

17

ABOUT VOLTS

'Fight her, Daniel! Fight!'

That's Si's voice saying that. And, despite what I said to Mary about surrendering, I decide I should at least try to defend myself. Somewhere inside my blasted brain, I put up my mental dooks and get ready to rumble.

But it's no good. Mary's spirit invades my mind like a bulldozer in a china shop and I'm simply barged to one side. In a second it's all over.

If my body is a spaceship, then Mary is now in the captain's seat, twiddling her fingers over the fancy buttons, wondering which one to try first.

And me? Well, weirdly, I'm still in there somewhere, squashed in a corner of my head, helpless. Mary becomes aware of me, and blasts at me again and again, but for some reason she can't get rid of me entirely. Maybe it's not possible to completely evict someone from their own brain. Not that it really matters. As far as my body's concerned, Mary is now calling all the shots.

As I watch, helpless, through eyes that used to be mine, I see my arms raise as Mary lifts her new hands to inspect them.

'Boy's fingers,' she says, wonder in her voice. 'On boy's hands. I'm alive again! And I'm a boy!'

Mary starts to chuckle. Then, from my tiny hiding place in the corner of what used to be my mind, I sense my whole body start to quake with triumphant laughter.

'I'm back! I'm alive! And this time I won't be pushed around. This time it will be different, so *different*...'

She raises her right arm and gestures into the air.

An arc of electricity springs from my – sorry, her finger tips, and explodes the peak of one of the Shard's spires with a BOOM of destruction. Amidst the roar of the wind and the sound of crashing glass, there is a piercing scream.

It's Mary, doing the screaming. Using my lungs and vocal cords, of course, but the pain is all hers. She raises the hand that just fired the electricity and we both see it is bloodied and charred.

Hey, that's mine! I shout out in my mind. I can't feel any pain now I've lost control of my body, but boy, that's gotta hurt! There's still smoke coming out of it.

'No,' gasps Mary aloud. 'It's mine! But it burns, aagh…!'

What did you expect? I shout again. *Living bodies and lightning don't exactly go together. You have to leave your powers behind, Mary. You can't use them now you're alive.*

'Silence!' Mary screams. 'This body is *mine!* But it's your fault if its flesh is weak. So, I will harden it with fire.' And she raises her hand again.

No! I shout, suddenly panicked. If I do ever find a way to get my body back, I'd like it to be returned in the condition I lent it out in, not charred to a crisp. But Mary isn't listening to me. She's too busy screaming as she flings a new bolt of electrical energy from my bloodied hand, taking out another chunk of the Shard. My hand is a blackened claw now, and my sleeve is on fire.

Oi! I shout. *You've damaged my coat!*

'I... don't understand...' Mary gasps through the pain.

You've won, Mary. I hate to admit this, but it's true. *You've got your new life, your second chance – take it. This is what you wanted, isn't it? Leave your spook powers behind, stop hurting people and just... live!*

Mary is on her knees now, sobbing. And that's not nice because all I can hear is me. Then she raises both her hands, and her whole body tenses.

Mary, what are you doing? Mary?

'Just... living isn't enough,' she says through gritted teeth. 'I need to be stronger than everyone else. Stronger even than grown men! I need this power for revenge...'

Mary, stop!

I can feel a massive electrical charge building around us now. Small arcs of energy are creeping up the remaining spires of the Shard and discharging into my body. My hair is standing on end, and the air feels like it will explode.

Mary!

'I will… make… this body… STRONG!' Mary gasps, and then screams a scream beyond anything I have ever heard before as she releases enough electrical power to light up Belgium. The summit of the Shard explodes as my body erupts into light.

And I'm a bit cross now. I mean, I basically gave her my body – and the rest of its life – for *free!* And here she is, a few seconds later, turning it into toast. All because she can't bear to give up her supernatural powers and accept normal life again.

Unfortunately, since the body of a fourteen-year-old boy isn't meant to be used as a light bulb, it looks like we're both about to die in its ashes. And for Mary, this'll be the second time.

Ah, crapsticks.

Well, at least I can't feel anything.

I only ever wanted to help you, I say in my head, while I still can. But Mary doesn't answer.

And that's when I notice she's gone.

From my mind, I mean. Gone! The captain's seat is vacant! In a moment I'm back in command of own dear mind and body again, and…

PAIN

Somehow I manage to open my eyes…

PAIN

I slump down onto my back, in a cloud of smoke and the smell of a badly singed psychic detective. My ruined, burnt-out fuse of a body won't move, but at least the electricity has left me now. Instead, it's lifting Mary's ghost up into the storm above, wreathing her in electrical fire. She reaches down to where I lie in the twisted ruins of the spires, but she's already too far away.

In fact, with the top of the building now completely destroyed, Mary can no longer be said to be on the Shard at all. And if Si – and the Great Poojam – are right that it's the building giving Mary all this extra power, then that means…

With a shocking suddenness, the electrical charge dissipates, and darkness falls over the summit of the Shard. The wind whistles through steel wreckage and shattered sheets of glass and ice. The snow swirls around Mary's ghost. She floats in the night sky above me, a slim teenage girl once again, with a look of sadness and confusion on her face.

As I watch, there's a sudden ripple in the ectoplasm of Mary's spirit. I recognise the signs.

'What's happening?' she says. 'I feel so… I feel… nothing.'

'You couldn't have what you wanted,' I manage to croak. 'In the end. A new life wasn't enough for you. Not if it had to be an ordinary one. So now there's nothing left to keep you here. You're free, Mary.'

'Free?'

'Wasn't that what you really wanted all along?'

'I'm fading?' she says, looking down at herself. She seems quite calm about it, but then they always are. 'Why am I fading?'

'I'm happy for you, Mary,' I say, still lying on the concrete platform. 'Really. It must have been horrible stuck here on earth all those years, after everything they did to you. But you can go now. To the Hereafter. You deserve it.'

Mary's ghostly hair ripples in an invisible wind that's got nothing to do with the weather. She's already getting hard to see.

'But what will I find there?'

I shrug. And yowzers, it hurts!

'I have no idea,' I say. 'That's not my department. But it's where we all go in the end. It's where you should be. Rest now, Mary. Goodbye.'

Mary's ghost looks at me.

'Dan,' she says, using my name for the first time. 'I'm so sorry.'

And she smiles – a proper, genuine, warm smile this time. It's the first time I've seen her do that too. Then the spectral wind takes the little wisp of golden light that remains of her ghost and whips it away to nothing.

'Ah, don't be,' I croak to the empty sky above. 'It's all in a night's work.'

Which is a pretty cool thing to say in the circs. Shame there's no one there to hear it.

'I'm here, Daniel.'

Si floats over me, looking distraught.

'That's good, Si.' I barely manage to whisper the words. 'Because I'm not sure I will be for much longer.'

And I close my eyes at last.

18

SIMON'S SECRET

DUBBA-DUBBA-DUBBA…
  That's a funny noise. But it does sound like something I've heard before.

DUBBA-DUBBA-DUBBA…

Then I remember that if I open my eyes, I might be able to see what it is.

I open my eyes.

'Daniel!'

I see Simon leaning over me, relief radiating out

147

from his ghastly face. The roof beyond him is curving and white, and there are boxy units of hi-tech kit and monitors.

DUBBA-DUBBA...

'Where am I?' I manage to whisper.

Before Simon can answer, a young woman in an orange jumpsuit marked 'paramedic' leans into view and says, 'You're in an air ambulance. Don't worry, you're going to be fine.'

So *that's* what the DUBBA-DUBBA is – the throb of helicopter blades.

Cool.

Then I remember what happened to put me in here.

'You came back for me, Si,' I croak up to my side-kick. 'Thanks, buddy.'

'Er...' says the woman in orange, who obviously thinks I'm talking to her. 'Just try to relax. You've had a double shot of morphine for the pain. If I were you, I'd try to get to some sleep.'

Simon waits for her to stop speaking before answering me.

'Of course I came back. I was never very far, Daniel, you should know that.'

'I'm sorry I said those things,' I say, remembering our argument in the ruined flat. 'I'm sorry I shouted.'

The paramedic says, 'Hey, I'd have shouted too if I'd been struck by lightning. That was one freak storm. It took the point of the Shard clean off.'

'It is I who should be sorry.' Si gives one of his most impressive bows, so I know he means it. 'I should never have lost faith in you, Daniel.'

'But you were right,' I say. 'About Mary. She really was too far gone. I wish I could have helped her, Si.'

We both look at the woman in orange, to see what she'll do. She shakes her head and looks away. I guess she thinks I'm just talking to myself, what with the shock of everything that's happened and the morphine, and all. And that suits me and Si just fine.

'But you *did* help her,' Simon says, now that we have the conversation to ourselves again. 'Against all the odds, you got her over to the Hereafter. That wouldn't have happened if you'd given up. And you saved Stacey and Ned. 'Tis a triumph, Daniel!'

'And Venn Specter?' I say. After everything that's happened, I find I'd like to have saved everyone, even the annoying star of Venn Specter Investigates.

'See for yourself,' says Si. 'For behold, the window of wonders!'

And he steps back, sweeping his arm towards a small TV screen in the corner of the air ambulance. It looks like the news is on, and – huddled in a silver foil blanket – Venn Specter is being interviewed.

'Ohmygodohmygod!' he says, his eyes wild. It looks like he might have thrown up a little on his bottle-green pullover. 'There was a ghost! An actual ghost! I can't believe it!'

'I'm sure your viewers would want me to ask, Mr Specter,' says the voice of an interviewer, 'why you seem so surprised to have seen a ghost? After all, your whole reputation has been built on your claim to be able to see ghosts all the time.'

'You don't understand.' Venn grabs the man by the lapels. 'It was a real ghost! And we got it on film. It was *recorded…*'

I tune out of the TV and look at Si, one eyebrow raised. After all, as far as I can tell, the whole crazy incident on the Shard was broadcast to the nation via Ned's camera. It must be causing an international sensation.

'As for that,' Simon says, with a mischievous grin. 'Ned's camera broadcast almost nothing.'

'But…' I blink at him. Even that hurts. 'What do you mean?'

'I don't pretend to understand your twenty-first century ways, Daniel, but the words "static" and "interference" are being used to explain it. The last thing that the audience saw on the big screen was a close-up of that keyring in the Shard's souvenir shop. After that, the picture went fuzzy. DazzleTV was forced to broadcast last year's *Venn Specter Investigates Christmas Special* instead.'

I can't help laughing. So much for Venn's precious proof. But I stop laughing when I feel the dull ache it causes throughout my body.

Then something glittery catches my eye, and I look back at the TV screen. There's a close up of Stacey there now, wiping her nose on the back of her hand.

'… you must have been very brave.' says the voice of the interviewer to Stacey. 'Did you see the ghost, too?'

'No, I saw a pretty lady,' says Stacey. 'And a weirdy boy. And the weirdy boy was jumping about and being funny. And there were sweeties. I want a sweety.'

There's the sound of laughter, and the shot zooms out to show Stacey's mum. Beside her are Tim and Ned.

'It was a terrible experience,' says Stacey's mum. 'I certainly won't be going to one of Venn Specter's shows again. I can only thank Mr Ned here for bringing my daughter back safe and sound.'

Ned gives the camera a polite nod, but says nothing.

'And the ghost?' The interviewer obviously doesn't want to let this point go.

'Well, I didn't see one,' says Stacey's mum. 'Just a terrible storm.'

I tune out again. It's tempting to think this is the end of Venn Specter and his low-down ways, but even as I think that, I know it won't be. Because in the end, he's right, isn't he? He's already a winner, because he's already famous. He'll find a way to turn all this to his advantage. After all, it's great publicity. I expect he'll have a book out by this time next year. And another series of his TV show.

I look back at the screen and, sure enough, the picture now shows Venn, still wrapped in foil, addressing his fans. In a way, it's even better for him that nothing was recorded. Now Venn can say whatever he likes. And from the size of the crowd, it looks like there are still plenty of people ready to believe him.

'Turn it off, Si.'

Simon bows, and then reaches his spectral hand into the television. It shuts down.

My body feels ready to do the same thing.

'How bad is it, Si?' I say. 'Me, I mean.'

'Well, you are a little crispy round the edges, but from what I heard the doctor say, most of you should make a full recovery.'

'Most of me?'

Simon looks a bit sheepish.

'Remind me, Daniel, are you left-handed or right-handed?'

I blink at him. Then I remember the sight of my right hand burnt to a blackened claw. I glance down at it now, and see that it's completely wrapped in bandages.

'I'm sure it's fine,' says Si, looking away. 'Well, I'm sure it's not as bad as it looks, anyway. Um…'

I look away too.

'Er, they did recover these,' Simon adds, lifting my purple specs with his spook powers. The paramedic is too busy trying to figure out why the TV has stopped working to notice. Si lowers them over my eyes. They're a bit wonky, but it feels good to be wearing them again. Then I remember something.

With my good hand I reach into my pocket and pull out the tatty old copy of *Wow TV* that Mrs Binns gave me. It already seems like a lifetime ago. I wave it feebly at Si.

'I've just realised something about this.'

Si looks confused.

'Look at the date on it,' I say, and drop the mag on my chest.

Simon looks. Then a solitary ectoplasmic cloud of understanding puffs out of the hole in his head. He glances up at me.

'This magazine's not just fourteen years old, Si,' I say. 'It's dated to the very week I was born. And I know enough about Mrs Binns to know that this isn't a coincidence.'

'Daniel…'

'Si, your secret's got something to do with my birth, hasn't it?'

Simon folds his arms, and looks out of the window. The DUBBA-DUBBA sound is different now, and I guess we're coming in to land. Si turns back at me.

'If I told you my secret, Daniel, it would not only explain why I am here with you, it would also turn your world upside down. I know you want answers, but what if those answers changed the very person you think you are? Are you really ready for that? As you lie there in a shattered body, with one arm reduced to charred bone…'

'You said it wasn't that bad!'

'… *one arm in a bandage,* I mean. In a *bandage.*' He looks flappy again. We feel the helicopter touch down.

'Look, Daniel. Please believe me when I say that I cannot tell you the secret today. Because if I did…'

'What, Si? Why can't you tell me?'

'… because, if I told you, it would be the start of the greatest and most dangerous adventure of your life.'

I stare at Si, and wonder how he can say such a thing after all that's just happened. But Simon says nothing more.

Then the door of the helicopter flies open, and I'm being rushed out on my trolley.

It's still snowing.

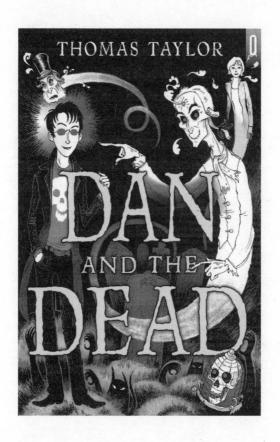

DAN AND THE DEAD

Dan talks to the dead – and helps solve their
problems. But when he takes on the case of a
teenage shoplifter, things spin out of control.

ISBN: 978 1 4081 5412 0   £5.99

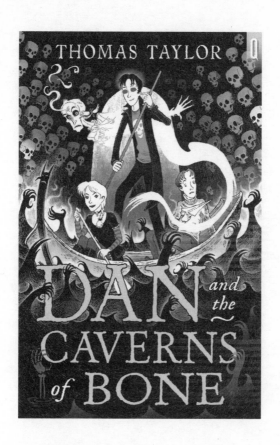

Dan and the
Caverns of Bone

The supernatural detective and his
ghostly sidekick find spooky
goings-on in the Paris catacombs

ISBN: 978 1 4081 7816 4   £5.99